THE STEPMOTHER

Rebecca's Story #1

BRENDA MAXFIELD

Tica House
Publishing

Sweet Romance that Delights and Enchants!

Personal Word from the Author

❦

Dearest Readers,

Thank you so much for choosing one of my books. I am proud to be a part of the team of writers at Tica House Publishing who work joyfully to bring you stories of hope, faith, courage, and love. Your kind words and loving readership are deeply appreciated.

I would like to personally invite you to sign up for updates and to become part of our **Exclusive Reader Club**—it's completely Free to join! We'd love to welcome you!

Much love,

Brenda Maxfield

VISIT HERE to Join our Reader's Club and to Receive Tica House Updates:

http://ticahousepublishing.subscribemenow.com

Chapter One

Behold, I will do a new thing; now it shall spring forth; shall ye not know it? I will even make a way in the wilderness, and rivers in the desert.

— ISAIAH 43:19 KJV

Rebecca bustled from the kitchen, balancing a platter of freshly-sliced homemade bread and two glasses filled with cold milk. She put them on the table and ran back for the other glasses of milk. When she'd gotten them plunked down, sloshing only a little, she stood back and surveyed her work.

Seven places set. Everything ready—except the large pot of stew, which she didn't want to take from the cooking stove until the van arrived. She bit the corner of her lip. Everything had to be perfect. She ran into the bathroom at the back of the house and peered into the small mirror above the sink.

Her cheeks were flushed bright red, and no matter how she tried to hide it, her eyes revealed her nervousness. She tried on a smile, but it looked as if she'd plastered it on with a knife. She took a huge, gulping breath and tried again. No. The smile was no good. She made a face into the mirror, and then chastised herself for being so proud as to be standing there practicing a smile. Goodness, when had she become so vain?

She turned away and went to the side door of the house, opening it and pushing the screen door to stick her head outside. The air nipped at her, but being only November, it hadn't grown too cold yet.

"Stephen! Stephen, come on in!" she hollered to her older brother. Stephen was married with a wife and baby daughter, but he'd traveled that day from Illinois to show his support to their father. Tabitha had stayed behind with little Nessy who had the sniffles.

Stephen emerged from the barn, wiping his hands on an old towel. "They're not here," he called back to her.

"Any minute now." She glanced toward the gravel drive which as of yet was completely empty of a van. But her father had sent word that they would be arriving shortly after noon that day. And when Rebecca had checked, it was already seven minutes after twelve.

Stephen walked over to her and clutched the handle of the screen. "You're nervous," he stated and then pushed past her into the house.

She followed him. "I know. I can't help it. We don't even know her, Stephen. What if I don't like her?"

He raised a brow. "You'll like her. If *Dat* liked her enough to marry her, then she has to be all right, *ain't so?*"

Rebecca shrugged. Maybe or maybe not.

"And three sons. Think on it. This house is going to be full," she continued.

Stephen gave her a strange look. "Three sons ain't nothing. What ails you? You're jumpier than I thought."

Rebecca stared at her brother, annoyed. "Wouldn't you be? What if it was you welcoming our new stepmother into your home? What if you were welcoming three new stepbrothers to live with you?" Rebecca glanced around the house. "I've been taking care of everything for as long as I can remember around here. It's going to be awful different."

Her voice faltered, and she swallowed back the sudden tears clogging her throat.

Her brother put his hand on her shoulder. "Ever think that maybe this is a *gut* thing? Ever think that maybe things will be better now?"

She blinked and tried to swallow. Her brother was right. Where was her faith? Where was her confidence in her dad? She shuddered and squared her shoulders.

"Lands sake, why are we standing around like fence posts anyway? I need to get the pot of stew on the table. You wash up."

She turned on her heel and fairly marched into the kitchen. *My kitchen,* she thought ruefully and pressed her lips together. Enough of that. Her dad was counting on her. She grabbed two hot pads and lifted the kettle from the cooking stove, walking carefully to the table with it. Even if the van didn't arrive from Linnow Creek for another fifteen minutes, the stew would surely hold its heat. She'd made it extra careful that day, cutting large chunks of stew meat, and not even thinking of conserving when she'd cut up potatoes and onions and carrots and emptied canned veggies into the stock.

She froze. *"Ach, nee!"*

Stephen poked his head out from the wash room. "What is it? What's happened?"

"I forgot to make the cornbread! Now, the meal is ruined! How in the world could I have forgotten?"

She threw the hot pads onto her plate and dashed back into the kitchen, whirling through the room, snatching ingredients from all the shelves. What was wrong with her? She always served up cornbread with stew. Her dad loved it and *expected* it. She ran to the gas fridge and grabbed three eggs. She closed the door with her hip and hurried to the counter.

"It ain't the end of the world, you know," Stephen said dryly from the door.

"No, it ain't, but *Dat* will be wondering at me. Wondering where my head is!"

She hurriedly began measuring out the ingredients, stirring like there was no tomorrow.

"Ach. The cooking stove."

Just then, the crunch of gravel was heard in the driveway. Rebecca crossed to the window and peered out. Sure enough, it was their regular Mennonite driver with his van, pulling in with a full load of passengers.

"Too late now," Stephen said. "Come on, Rebecca. Don't fret. Let's go meet our new family."

Rebecca stood very still. They had arrived. For six months, her dad had been traveling back and forth to Linnow Creek, courting the widow Amelia. Not once had Rebecca met her. She hadn't even traveled to Linnow Creek for the wedding. Her father had told her that she couldn't leave her goats that long. Nor the rest of the animals. In truth, his willingness to cut her out of the celebration hurt.

Why couldn't they have gotten their neighbors to watch the goats —to milk them and feed them? And the chickens and the cow and horses? It would have only been for a night or two. The Guths down the road would have been happy to oblige, but Rebecca hadn't pushed it. She'd been so stunned by her father's attitude that she had just nodded and gone along with it.

Now, she regretted it. She should have insisted on joining her dad— but a daughter insisting something contrary to her father's wishes wasn't done.

Stephen and his wife had been all right with missing the ceremony. Neither he nor his wife had been inclined to take a trip with their five-month-old baby. Stephen was content with just coming to Hollybrook alone and meeting Amelia and her boys here.

And her brother Amos?

Rebecca swallowed past the sudden lump in her throat. Amos was a different story entirely. Her heart gave its usual lurch at the thought of her lost brother.

"You coming?" Stephen asked.

Rebecca gave a start and shook herself from her thoughts. "*Jah, jah*. Of course."

Chapter Two

Rebecca hurried out to the front porch and stood at the top step beside Stephen. The van had stopped at the base of the stairs. Her father Noah got out of the front seat. He opened the sliding door at the side of the van, and three young boys clambered out. Rebecca gave a welcoming smile and went down the steps to greet them.

They all stood in a row, staring at her with identical pairs of wide blue eyes. Their various shades of blonde hair were all cut in even bowl cuts. The little one's hair was smooshed to one side as if he'd been leaning against the window the entire ride there.

They were adorable, and her heart warmed at the sight of them.

And then, *she* got out—her father's new wife. Rebecca's new stepmother. The young woman didn't look all that much older than she was. But Rebecca knew Amelia was twenty-seven, as she had asked her father. But right then, the woman's look of nervousness and almost fear caught at Rebecca's throat, making her new stepmother look not more than twenty-one or twenty-two. Rebecca's trepidation lessened, and she stepped forward to greet her kindly.

But in that quick flash of a moment, the woman's expression flipped to a look of bravado and confidence. She pulled her apron more tightly over her ample bosom and gave Rebecca a look of distinct superiority.

"*Gut* afternoon," she said crisply. "I am your *dat's* new wife."

Rebecca bit the corner of her lip, not knowing how to react. She'd just witnessed such a contrast in expressions that she was left temporarily off-balance.

"Hello," Stephen interjected. "It's nice to finally meet you. I'm Stephen, the eldest."

The woman nodded. "Hello. Of course, I'm Amelia." She trained her hazel eyes back on Rebecca. "Your new stepmother."

Rebecca put her smile back on. "Nice to meet you."

"And these are my boys. Your new step-brothers." Amelia gestured toward the boys who were still, miraculously, standing there in a straight unmoving line. "My eldest is Alex, he's eight. Next is Michael, seven, and young William, five. Boys, greet your new brother and sister."

The boys looked as if they'd rather be anywhere else in the world, but they obediently offered their greetings.

Rebecca's smile turned genuine. "Hello, lads. Right nice to meet you."

Stephen grinned. "Maybe, we'll go fishing the next time I come around to Hollybrook."

That got a smile from the oldest and the youngest. Michael seemed to be reserving judgement.

By then, her father and the driver had gotten all the luggage from the back of the van and put it on the porch. Stephen stepped forward and Rebecca heard him making arrangements with the driver to be picked up early the next morning to travel back to his home just over the border into Illinois.

"The meal ready?" Noah asked Rebecca.

Rebecca nodded. "It's on the table." She glanced at her new family. "Come on in," she said. "You can get washed up, and we'll sit right down."

If she wasn't mistaken, Rebecca thought she saw Amelia bristle at her suggestion, but she had to have been mistaken. Why would the offer of a hot meal bother her? Amelia turned to her boys and said, "Boys, go get washed up now," as if Rebecca suggesting they do so wasn't adequate somehow.

Tread lightly, Rebecca silently warned herself.

Her dad and Stephen grabbed up half of the suitcases. "Won't the meal be cold?" her dad asked her as they all started inside. "How long has it been on the table?"

Rebecca stared at him. Never in all the years since her mother's death when she'd taken over the running of the household, had her father questioned whether the food would be appropriately hot. He must have realized the same thing, for he coughed roughly and frowned.

"I'm sure it's fine," he said, clearly trying to change his tune. "Thank you for preparing it."

"You're welcome," Rebecca muttered, knowing at that moment just how much her entire life was about to change.

After everyone had washed up, they came to the table. Rebecca stood aside while her father decided where everyone would sit. She had been relegated out of her usual spot to the other side of the table. She wasn't surprised, knowing that Amelia would of course want to take her spot as Noah's wife. For years, Rebecca had sat beside Noah after serving the food. But now, Amelia sat in her place, perched awkwardly, her plump arms resting on the edge of the table.

"Let's bow for the blessing," her father said.

Everyone bowed, and during the silence, Rebecca prayed fervently for God's help and direction as they all settled into what would be their new life. When her dad cleared his throat, everyone looked up, the silent blessing over. Rebecca stood, ready to ladle the stew. Amelia reached for the ladle and snatched it up before Rebecca's fingers could touch it. Rebecca's cheeks flamed hot, and she sank back onto the bench, the message received.

Noah seemed oblivious to the tension between his daughter and his new wife. Rebecca gazed at him, noting how relaxed he looked. She saw how the wrinkles around his eyes had smoothed out. How his mouth, above the long scraggly beard that reached to his chest, was poised with a ready smile. She blinked. He was happy. Perhaps happier than she ever remembered seeing him.

Her breath seeped out in a long quiet sigh. Well, then. She was going to do her utmost to ensure that this transition went as smoothly as possible. She smiled at the boys sitting across from her. Alex returned her smile. The middle one, Michael, still looked to be contemplating his opinion of the entire situation. And William looked positively spooked. *Poor little guy,* Rebecca thought. He looks about how I feel. She nearly giggled out loud, but she caught herself in time. There was no way she would be able to explain her laughter. She winked at him, and his eyes widened, but he quickly averted his gaze.

No matter, she thought. *We're going to become friends. You wait and see.*

Chapter Three

After the meal, Rebecca was at the sink in the kitchen, washing up the dishes. Amelia ladled the left-over stew into glass jars to store in the refrigerator.

"The meal was tasty," her new stepmother told her in a voice that sounded almost grudging.

Rebecca turned from the sink. "Thank you, Amelia."

Amelia licked her lips and put down the ladle. She moved closer to the sink. "There's, uh, there's something I want to ask you."

"*Jah?*"

"Your *dat* won't talk much about Amos."

Rebecca stiffened. That was no surprise. Her father rarely if ever mentioned Amos's name. She shifted her weight from one foot to the other. She didn't feel right talking about her brother Amos with Amelia. Wasn't that up to her father? She looked into Amelia's eyes, seeing her interest. Rebecca wanted to be friends with this woman who was—in a way—pushing her out of her place in this household. She wanted things to be pleasant between them.

If she refused to discuss Amos, would Amelia resent her for it? Would it make things difficult and awkward between them?

"What did *dat* say?" Rebecca ventured, trying to feel out just exactly what Amelia did know.

"That he's nineteen," Amelia answered.

Rebecca waited, but Amelia said no more. She inhaled sharply. Was that all Amelia knew? His age? Was that *all* her father had told his new wife? That seemed surprising even considering the situation. Rebecca glanced toward the door, wondering where her father was. Had he taken the boys outside? Was Stephen out there with them?

Rebecca didn't want to be disloyal. Yet in all fairness, Amelia should know more about Amos than his age.

Amelia sighed. "You won't tell me something else?" she asked, and again Rebecca saw a look on her face that made her appear young and vulnerable. But again, the look quickly disappeared. Amelia drew herself up and raised her chin. "Fine."

"I-I s'pose I could tell you a bit more..." Rebecca took her hands out of the water and grabbed the hand towel from the counter.

"If it's a problem, never mind," Amelia said, her voice crisp.

"I just don't want to tell you—"

Amelia raised a hand. "I understand. He's your *dat*. I'm just some woman he married." She spun on her heel, turning back to the half-filled jars of stew.

Rebecca walked to the table where Amelia was working. "It's not that..."

Amelia shrugged. "It doesn't matter. Forget I asked."

"He ran off," Rebecca said abruptly. "We don't know where he is." Even speaking the words made Rebecca's heart cringe. Even after a whole year, it still almost seemed unreal to her.

Amelia looked at her. "You don't?"

Rebecca swallowed. "*Nee*. We don't know."

"Is he shunned?"

"*Nee*. He never joined church. But, he's as *gut* as shunned."

"What did he do?"

Rebecca shook her head slowly. What *didn't* Amos do? He had a rebellious streak a mile long. He had begun acting out even before his *Rumspringa*. He couldn't wait to run around with the *Englisch*. And not just any *Englisch*, but the boys who were involved with fast cars and faster girls. The boys who were on the fringes of their own society. Amos had taken to them like a duck to a pond.

Tears burned her eyes as she remembered the continual harsh words between her father and Amos. The fighting. The constant discord. Rebecca used to cower in her room, hearing the yelled words through the walls. Her older brother Stephen had been lucky. He was often gone in the evenings courting Tabitha. After he wed, he was able to avoid all of it by moving to Illinois. Now and again, he'd ask Rebecca how it was between their father and Amos. Rebecca would always burst into tears, hardly able to talk about it.

Just as she could hardly talk about it right then with Amelia.

"Well?" Amelia asked.

"He, uh, he spent a lot of time with the *Englisch*."

Amelia grimaced. "A lot of our young men do during *Rumspringa*."

"He used to drive their cars. Once..." she paused, feeling as if she were betraying both her brother and her father by speaking.

"Once what?" Eagerness edged Amelia's words.

"Well, once he got into trouble," Rebecca said, not wanting to share all the facts anymore. This wasn't right. She shouldn't be sharing this information. It was her dad's place to do it, not hers.

"What kind of trouble?"

"I think *Dat* should tell you," Rebecca said. "I'm sure he'll want to..." Her voice faded. She wasn't sure at all.

"So, you won't say no more?"

"I'm sorry, Amelia, truly, but I think *Dat*—"

Again, Amelia raised her hand, stopping Rebecca. "We'll see what he tells me," she said curtly. "Forget I asked."

And with that, she left the room, the jars not yet filled and now forgotten.

Rebecca watched her go. She wouldn't say Amelia stormed from the room exactly, but her stepmother was definitely annoyed. Why in the world hadn't her dad shared more about his second son? Amelia was his wife now, so surely, she had the right to know. And now, thanks to the whole situation, she and Amelia had gotten off to a bad start.

Rebecca finished filling the jars with the leftover stew and tucked them into the refrigerator. Then she finished washing up the dishes. When the kitchen was completely *red* up, she walked out to the porch to see where everyone was. Alex came running out of the barn, his face alight, chasing one of her goats. It was Jasmine, the most stubborn goat she owned, but one of her best milkers. She hardly wanted Alex to be playing tag with the animal.

"Wait!" she called, hurrying down the steps and running toward them. "Don't chase her!"

But Alex either didn't hear her or didn't choose to hear her, Rebecca wasn't sure. She raced after the boy, catching up with him as he circled the barn toward the hen house.

"Alex!"

This time, he did stop. *"Jah?"*

"That's Jasmine. She's full of mischief," Rebecca said, grabbing her breath. "She's a *gut* milker, so I let her be."

"You milk them goats?" Alex asked, his eyes wide with interest.

"Twice a day. Morning and night. Some folks only milk their goats once a day, but I do it twice. They produce more, and they're used to it now."

"So, that's why you got so many?"

Rebecca laughed. "We only have nine. And one Billy goat." She pointed to a pen not far from the hen house. "We keep him separated from the nannies. Unless we're wanting some kids."

"Can I milk 'em?"

Rebecca gazed at him. "Would you like to learn?"

He nodded vigorously. "We never had no goats. Chickens and cows. And horses, of course."

"We sell the milk."

"You do? And get money for it?"

She smiled. "*Jah*, we get money for it."

"Then I for sure want to learn how." Alex leaned closer to her. "Don't be letting Michael or William help. They're too little."

Rebecca bit back a laugh. She knew for a fact that Alex only had one year on Michael. "Are they, now?"

He nodded. "Michael's mad, anyway."

They were walking toward the Billy goat's pen. Gotthard was staring at them with his slitted eyes, his beard brushing against the metal fence. Jasmine was nowhere to be seen.

"Why's Michael mad?"

"He don't want to be here. He likes it in Linnow Creek."

"How about you? You mad, too?"

His face crinkled. "What do I got to be mad for? I'm getting a new *dat*, ain't I?"

Rebecca's brow rose. "Indeed, you are. And a new sister to boot," she added.

He put his hand in hers, startling her. But she curled her fingers around his, and they continued to the pen. Rebecca made the introductions.

"Gotthard, huh? That's a dumb name," Michael observed.

Rebecca grinned. "*Jah*, it kind of is. I don't even know where the name came from. Come to think of it, I think the people we bought this goat from had already named him."

Alex stuck his finger through the fence and petted Gotthard's nose. "Well, it's still a dumb name."

Chapter Four

That night, Rebecca lie in bed listening. For so long, she and her *dat* had been the only ones in the house at night. Now, there was a house full. She heard the floor boards in the hallway creaking as little feet headed back and forth to the bathroom. She heard a low rumble of conversation coming from her father's room. She even heard Stephen snoring from the room just down on her right.

So odd. She thought it'd be nice to have the house full, but instead, all the sounds of life seemed out of place, as if taunting her to adjust. Or perhaps, they were warning her that life would never be the same. She threw her covers off and padded over to her window. She pulled aside the white curtains and peered outside. The moon was full, and its light fell over the still yard, casting shadows of the naked trees onto the ground. She stared up into the sky, looking at the stars and wondering how far away they really were.

In seventh grade, they'd studied the stars, but only enough to leave Rebecca curious and wanting to know more. She'd gone to the public library in Hollybrook and checked out a few books on the heavenly bodies. When her dad had seen the books, he'd scoffed, telling her that she'd do a lot better studying things on the earth. Like farming and gardening and raising her goats.

She'd taken the books to her room them, only reading them in private. She could learn about farming and such from her father, but he couldn't teach her about the stars, and she wanted to know. But life and chores had gotten in the way, and she never did finish reading those books. They were due before she'd read them all, and she had to take the books back.

Only later did she learn that you could re-check books out for a longer period of time. But by then, she had discovered fiction, and she was busy delving into new and strange worlds through make-believe characters. Those books, she also kept in her room, unsure whether her father would approve or not. When she felt guilty about it, she simply started reading again, and before long she was so caught up in the pretend worlds that her guilt dissipated into nothing.

Now, she smiled at the twinkling lights in the sky, pressing her fingers on the window glass. Some people thought that other creatures lived on different planets, which she knew was silly. But still, it did give fodder for the imagination.

"Stop it!" came a small voice from the hallway.

She hurried across her room and opened the door. Michael and William stood there, glaring at each other in the candlelight.

"What's happened?" Rebecca asked.

"Nothin'," said Michael. "We was just going back to bed."

The candle in his hand was steady as he tromped down the hall toward their bedroom. William scurried after him, and they both disappeared. Rebecca was about to step back into her own room, when her father's bedroom door opened and Amelia poked her head out.

"What's that noise?" she asked.

"The boys were just going back to bed. They probably had to use the toilet."

Amelia's expression tightened. She held her candle high and peered down the hall. "So, they're back in bed?"

"*Jah*. I'm sure they are."

Amelia looked about to say something further but must have changed her mind. Instead, she gave Rebecca a long look and then ducked her head back inside the room and the door closed.

Rebecca hesitated a moment. And then, with a sigh, she went back to bed, too.

~

Early the next morning, Stephen stood on the porch waiting for the van driver. Rebecca stood beside him even though she needed to be inside, starting the eggs for breakfast.

"I'm glad you came," she said. "It was right nice to have you. I wish you could have brought Tabitha and Nessy."

"Next time," he said. "Tabitha wasn't too keen on missing out on a visit with you, either."

"Give them both a hug for me."

"I will." Stephen looked at her. "You going to be all right?"

His question startled her. "Of course. I'm fine."

"It's going to be different around here."

There's an understatement, she thought. "*Jah*, it is."

"But you'll be okay?"

"I'm fine, Stephen."

He nodded slowly, looking as if he didn't quite believe her. Rebecca tried to smooth out her features. She must look worried to cause Stephen's concern. If the truth were known, she *was* worried. She didn't know what her place was anymore.

"I'll have Tabitha write you. She can tell you what Nessy's up to. We're looking for her to sit up by herself right soon."

"That'll be a help."

Stephen chuckled. "That it will."

The gravel crunched as the white van turned into the drive.

"Well, here's my ride."

"Did you say *gut*-bye to *Dat?*"

"I did. He's out in the barn."

Rebecca nodded. Behind her, in the house, she heard rustling. Amelia was up, and likely, the boys weren't too far behind. The van pulled to a stop in front of the porch. Stephen picked up his small bag, smiled his farewell to Rebecca, and got into the van. Within a minute, he was on his way. Rebecca remained on the porch for a moment, watching the van disappear down the road. Then she took a bracing breath and went inside the house.

Amelia was in the kitchen, warming the cast iron skillet on the cook stove. She looked over when Rebecca entered.

"*Gut* morning," she said.

Rebecca nodded. "Morning. Stephen has just left. I was fixin' to get the eggs fried up."

"No need. I'll do it." Amelia reached for the glass bowl full of eggs.

"I'll start the toast. The bacon is already fried."

"I smelled it when I came down." Amelia gave her a strange look. "I want you to know that I'll be getting up earlier after this."

"Don't worry about it," Rebecca said, trying to offer her some comfort. "You've just moved houses and districts. That's a lot of change."

Amelia frowned. "Still, I'll be getting up earlier."

Rebecca said no more. It was odd having another woman in the house. Just as it was odd that they weren't that far apart in years. It was doubly odd that this woman was her dad's new wife who came with three children. The whole thing was going to take some getting used to. Rebecca peered out the window and saw her dad coming in from the barn. He was walking faster than normal, and she wondered if something had happened out there.

As he drew closer, she saw a look of excitement on his face. Normally, she only saw that look when one of their animals had just given birth. Other than that, his expression was quite sober. It was

November and none of their animals were pregnant, much less ready to give birth. She continued to watch him, almost expecting him to break out into a skip or a hop.

He came in the side door, and with him, a swirl of cold air wafted into the kitchen. She put down the bread she was buttering and went to meet him. He emerged from the wash room, rubbing his hands together.

"Cold out there?" she asked, already knowing it was from standing out there with Stephen.

Her father answered, "Not bad. Breakfast ready?"

She was taken aback by his question. Was that why he was there? He never came in asking if breakfast was ready. She always called him in. Nor did he come bounding in with such a smile on his face. And then it hit her—he was happy. Marrying Amelia had changed him in ways she didn't think possible. She was glad for him. But a sense of not belonging anymore filled her again, and she shoved it aside.

"Amelia and I are working on it."

Her father peered around her toward the kitchen. "She in there?"

"*Jah, Dat.* She's in there." She couldn't help but grin.

He nodded and tugged on his beard, but he didn't go in. Instead, he headed for the dining room. Rebecca went back into the kitchen to continue getting breakfast ready. Amelia had to have heard her father come in, but she said nothing. Nor did she go to look for him. However, her cheeks appeared slightly flushed, and Rebecca thought she saw the hint of a smile tugging at her lips.

Chapter Five

During the middle of the morning, Old Mae—the healer in their district—came to call. Rebecca hurried out to the porch to welcome her in.

"Old Mae! How nice to see you. What brings you out this morning?"

The wizened old woman walked up the steps with surprising agility for someone her age. "I heard Noah brought home his bride yesterday."

"That he did. And her three boys."

"I'll be wanting to meet them."

"Come on in. I'll put on some tea."

Rebecca ushered her into the house and went right to the kitchen to make tea. Amelia was upstairs, organizing the boys' room, and must not have heard Old Mae's arrival, for she didn't come down. Old Mae followed Rebecca into the kitchen.

"The Eashes are back. Did you hear?" Old Mae commented.

Rebecca turned from the faucet where she was filling the kettle. "What? Luke and Olivia Eash are back?" Her pulse quickened at the thought. They'd been gone for, what was it, at least five years. Rebecca didn't think they'd ever come back.

"*Jah*, child, they're back. It's right nice to think of them as part of us again."

Rebecca remembered their twin boys, Liam and Levi, who were older than her by about seven or eight years. And Eve. She smiled. She and Eve had been close friends in the third and fourth grades, before the Eashes left the district. She wondered if Eve was married now, or if she'd moved back to Hollybrook with them.

"Did all of them come?" she asked.

Old Mae ran a hand over her wrinkled chin. "I ain't for sure and for certain, but I think it's just Liam and Eve who's come with their folks. I plan to stop over as soon as I'm done here."

Rebecca's heart beat a bit faster. Eve was back. Perhaps they could rekindle their old friendship. They had both intended to write when they were split apart, and indeed, they had for a few months. But things had tapered off to nothing not long after that. Rebecca was never sure why; she supposed life just got in the way.

Old Mae glanced through the kitchen door. "Now, I'm wanting to meet the new wife and the three boys."

Rebecca turned on the burner under the kettle. She dropped

teabags into three cups. "I'll go fetch Amelia right now. I think the boys might be outside, but I'm not certain."

Old Mae sank into a rocker. "I'll wait here."

Rebecca scurried from the kitchen and hurried up the stairway. She found Amelia in the boys' room, putting clothes into the dresser.

"Amelia, Old Mae is here to meet you."

"Old Mae?"

"She's the healing woman in the district. She knows everything about herbs and tonics."

Amelia straightened and then patted her hair beneath her *kapp*. "*Gut*. I was wanting to make her acquaintance."

She followed Rebecca down the stairs, but when they got close to the kitchen, Amelia bustled ahead to enter first.

"*Gut* morning," she said with a wide smile.

"So, you're the new wife," Old Mae replied.

Rebecca went to take the honey down from the shelf.

"I am. Uh, I have three boys."

"That I know."

"Would you like to meet them?"

"All in *gut* time. Sit down here by me, and let's talk a bit."

The kettle started to hum, and Rebecca took it off the burner and poured steaming water into the three cups she'd prepared. She put a dollop of honey in each and stirred them a bit. Then she carried one to Old Mae and Amelia and took the third herself.

Old Mae gave Rebecca a long look. "Can you be finding the boys for us?"

Rebecca stood again from where she'd just sat at the work table. Was she being dismissed? Old Mae was nothing if not direct. "I'll run outside and find them."

She slipped out of the kitchen into the wash room. Since it was nearly winter, she supposed she should put shoes on. She preferred to go barefoot, as she did all spring and summer. Most of the fall, too, if the truth were known. By November, the Indiana ground sometimes grew painfully cold. Best she not even try that day. She pulled on the thick socks she kept stuffed in her sturdy black shoes that were waiting for her by the door. Then she put on her shoes and tied the laces. Grabbing a shawl from a peg, she hurried outside and went straight to the barn.

Inside, her father was bent over a plow, with all three boys looking on. It appeared that he was teaching them how to sharpen the blade.

"Excuse me, *Dat*," she said, walking close.

Noah Riehl looked up, seeming surprised to see her. "Hello, daughter."

"Old Mae has come to call."

"I thought I heard a buggy."

"She wants to meet the boys."

Noah straightened up from his bent position and stretched and rolled his shoulders. "Well, we can't keep Old Mae waiting, now, can we?"

He ruffled Alex's hair and grinned.

"Who's Old Mae?" Michael asked, his mouth puckering into a sour look.

"She's a mighty necessary woman in these parts," Noah answered. "Come on. Let's go in."

They all traipsed to the house behind Rebecca.

"You want some tea, *Dat?*" she asked, opening the door. She figured the water would still be warm.

"Sounds right *gut.*"

They all shed their shoes in the wash room and went into the kitchen. Amelia made introductions, and all of them sat around the work table. Rebecca stood by the sink, watching. Suddenly, Amelia sprang up and went to the counter, opening the cookie jar. She grabbed a plate and took out some of the oatmeal raisin cookies Rebecca had made a few days before. She piled them on a plate and offered them to everyone. The boys each snatched one and began happily munching. Old Mae declined, but her father took two.

Rebecca had the odd feeling of being an observer in her own life. Almost as if she'd floated up somewhere and was watching a performance. She should have been the one to offer the cookies. She had been the hostess in that old farmhouse for years. But now it was Amelia doing her job. A sense of unrest filled her, unlike the whispers of it the day before. Today, it was a much stronger sensation, more pervasive.

She watched her dad laugh at something Old Mae said. She watched both Alex and William staring at her dad as if they couldn't get enough of him. They were all one big happy family. Where did that leave her? She blinked hard and gave herself a silent scolding. What was wrong with her? She was acting like a spoiled child. Did she really begrudge any of them their new happiness?

They were her family now. All of them except Old Mae. Funny, though. She felt like Old Mae was more a part of her than these strangers.

Give it time... The words echoed in her brain, and she clung to them. Just what had she expected, anyway? For Amelia and the boys to move right in and everything to be normal? Rebecca turned toward the sink and washed the spoon she'd used with the honey. And then, with no one noticing, she slipped out of the kitchen.

Chapter Six

Old Mae was long gone, and the noon meal had been served, eaten, and cleared away. Rebecca had gone out to the barn to spend some time with her goats. In truth, they didn't need her attention, but she loved being with them. She enjoyed the crisp fall air and seeing the puffs of steam her breath made. The goats crowded around her as they always did whenever she was near.

"*Nee*, it ain't milking time," she said, laughing. She rubbed Jasmine between her horns. "Nor feeding time. Don't you worry. I'll be back out this evening. I'm just here to pass a few minutes."

From his pen outside the barn, Gotthard bleated. Rebecca always imagined that his loud, raucous protests could be heard miles away. She had no proof of this, however, as she'd never heard him from that far. Still, his bleating could drill holes in a person's ears.

"You hear that?" Rebecca asked her small herd of nannies. "You hear him? Complaining again. I guess I'll have to go out and give him some attention, too."

Young Frizzle, so named because of the curly lock of hair between his ears, jumped up on her, his hooves easily reaching her shoulders.

"Frizzle, you get on down. Goodness, you'll get me all dirty!" She laughed again, feeling lighter and happier than she had all day.

"Becca?" came a soft voice from the barn door.

Rebecca whirled and saw Eve Eash. It had to be Eve—she had the same dark brown hair and the same crooked front teeth. But she was taller. Much taller.

"Eve?"

Eve nodded, grinning. Rebecca rushed to her and gave her a quick hug.

"You're back! Old Mae told us that your family had returned. Where are you living? Do you still own your old place? Goodness, but you've grown tall!" The words tumbled from Rebecca's mouth. "*Ach,* but it's *gut* to see you."

"I'm glad we're back," Eve said. "I never wanted to leave in the first place."

"That was ages ago. How are you?"

Eve smiled. "I'm fine."

But there was something about her tone that said otherwise. Rebecca searched her friend's face, but decided to honor her privacy. Eve would tell her later if something was wrong.

"Come into the house. I'll make tea." Rebecca pushed through the goats, who were now surrounding both her and Eve. "Go on now," she told them. "I'll be back later."

"Land's sake, you've got a lot of goats."

"Not so many. Eight nannies and one Billy goat. I sell the milk and make some cheese. Not much, but enough to bring in some money." She put her hand on Eve's elbow. "Come on."

They walked to the side door of the house. Surely Amelia wouldn't mind if she brought a friend in for tea. They took their shoes off in the wash room and headed to the kitchen. Amelia wasn't about, and Rebecca got straight to making tea.

"Sit down, and tell me how your family is."

Another shadow crossed Eve's face, but it was quickly replaced by a pleasant expression.

"We're all fine. *Mamm* and *Dat* and Liam moved back with me. And yes, we still own the farm. *Dat* had been leasing it out all these years." She crinkled her nose. "The house doesn't look the same, though. The people *Dat* leased it to were hard on it. *Mamm* about had a fit. But Liam is already working on repairs."

"It was the Stuckeys who lived there. I thought they'd bought it from you. They left a couple months ago, I think. Private people. No one knew them much."

Eve shuddered and focused back on Rebecca. "Anyway, Liam will have it fixed up in no time. You remember him, don't you?"

Rebecca gave her a warm smile. "Of course, I do. Both Liam and Levi." Her cheeks grew warm. She'd had a major crush on both boys when she was young. But if she'd had to choose, she'd always liked Liam best. "So, Levi didn't move back with you?"

Eve's face clouded. "*Nee*," was all she said.

Odd, thought Rebecca; but again, she didn't pry. Levi probably had a family of his own by then.

"Well, I'm glad you're back. Do you want to go with me to the Youth Singing this Sunday evening?'

Eve tilted her head. "I suppose."

"Reuben Yoder is leading it this time, and he always chooses the faster songs. You'll like it."

"All right. I'll go with you."

"*Gut.* And the Yoders almost always serve ice cream."

Eve smiled. "Sounds fine."

"Hello."

Rebecca turned to see Amelia in the kitchen doorway. "Amelia, this is my old friend Eve. Eve Eash. Her parents and her brother have moved back into the district."

Amelia stepped forward. "You were away?"

Eve nodded. "For quite a while. Nice to meet you." She glanced at Rebecca, and Rebecca saw the questions in her eyes. Eve knew that she had no sisters or any other female in the house.

"Amelia is my *dat's* new wife. She has three boys, so now I have five brothers."

Eve didn't blink an eye at this news, for which Rebecca was

grateful. Eve had to notice that Amelia was hardly older than they were.

"Wait ... Did you say Eash?" Amelia asked, her face draining of all color.

"*Jah.* I'm Eve Eash."

Amelia visibly swallowed. "Well, it's right nice to meet you," she said, now in a seeming hurry. "Uh, excuse me, I have some chores that need doing." And just like that, she was gone.

Rebecca stared after her, wondering what was wrong. She didn't know Amelia, but she certainly knew what an upset person looked like. Why in the world would meeting Eve cause such a reaction? She turned to Eve, who looked just as perplexed.

"Amelia and her boys just moved in," Rebecca said by way of explanation. "We're all getting used to each other."

Eve nodded. "Where is she from? I don't remember her from when we lived here."

"*Nee*, you wouldn't. She was living in Linnow Creek, in our Amish district there. She moved here with *Dat.*"

"She seemed... Well, she seemed upset."

Rebecca looked over her shoulder in the direction Amelia had left. "That she did." She shrugged. "A lot to get used to, *ain't so?*"

Eve looked thoughtful.

"Here's your tea." Rebecca sat down with her at the table. They both sipped the warm liquid, and Rebecca started to giggle.

"Remember that time Tommy yanked on your apron and you turned and gave him a kick?"

Eve's cheeks colored. "Don't know what got into me. Imagine. Kicking someone."

"The teacher wasn't pleased, that was for sure and for certain."

Eve laughed. "First and last time I ever kicked anyone. Did you know Deacon Elias was sent to see me?" She whistled under her breath. "I was scolded but *gut*."

Rebecca grinned. "It wasn't funny, but it was."

They stared at each other and burst into laughter.

"The look on Tommy's face! It was like the earth had stopped spinning."

Eve leaned close. "He never did yank on my clothes again. Hmm. Don't think he ever spoke to me again neither. He still around?"

Rebecca shook her head. "He moved to Ohio about four years back. Married a girl over there. Heard he already has three kinner, too."

"Well, *gut* for him," Eve said, still chuckling.

"Why'd you come back?"

Eve grew pensive and took her time before answering. "*Dat* and *Mamm* always missed Hollybrook. Rover's Corner was nice enough, but it never felt like home."

Rebecca could feel the sorrow behind Eve's words.

"And my brother, Levi, well..." Her voice faded.

"What? Is he all right? Did he stay in Illinois?"

"We don't rightly know where Levi is."

Rebecca's eyes widened. "What happened?"

"I think *Dat* was hoping we'd find him here, back in Hollybrook. He took off during his *Rumspringa* and, well, he never came back."

"You don't hear from him?"

"*Nee*." Eve's eyes welled with tears. "Not even Liam does. And him and Levi was always so close. You know how twins are. Closer than most."

Rebecca nodded. "I'm sorry."

Eve shook herself, blinking away her tears. "How's your family been?"

"Stephen is married now. He's in Illinois, but not around Rover's Corner. He's up north. His wife's name is Tabitha and they have a *boppli*, Nessy."

"I always remember Stephen as being right nice. I'm glad he's married and has a family."

"He's happy. You just missed seeing him. He was here to see *Dat* and Amelia after the wedding."

"And wasn't your other brother named Amos? Is he married?"

Rebecca's chest tightened. "I don't know. He's like your Levi."

"*Ach.* I'm sorry. He left during *Rumspringa?*"

Rebecca's shook her head. "Not exactly. He ran away a lot. But I guess the last time was during *Rumspringa*."

"It's hard, *ain't so?* I pray for Levi all the time." She shrugged. "It's hard to see the pain in *Mamm's* eyes. *Dat* is just mad about it. But *Mamm*..."

"It's hard."

"That it is." Her voice was soft.

They were silent for a long moment, each lost in their own thoughts. The side door slammed shut and both girls gave a start.

"*Mamm!*" came Michael's voice. "Where are you?"

Rebecca smiled. "That's one of my new brothers. Come on, and I'll introduce you."

Chapter Seven

Liam ran his hand over the leather straps on the bridle. They were well worn. In fact, they ought to be replaced. He hung the bridle back up on the nail and looked about the barn. He remembered it well from his childhood, but back then, it had seemed so much larger. Now, as an adult, it looked to be of medium size. Big enough for their needs, anyway.

He walked to the corner of the barn where there was a workbench. A low shelf, cluttered with various tools, ran along the wall above the bench. Maybe he could set up a leather shop there. It'd be mighty cold when the dead of winter set in, but still, it would be a start. With a year of good crops, maybe he could build a shop on the property—there was plenty of room for one.

He picked up a heavy, rusted anvil and turned it over in his hands. Had their last renter shod horses? He set it back down, stifling feelings of impatience. He didn't want to be back in Hollybrook. Not really. Things had been going well in Rover's Corner. His leather work shop did a decent business, and he'd have liked to keep it going. When his folks first started talking about returning to Hollybrook, he'd been sure they were joking.

But when his dad started talking about their Levi, and how he might have returned to Indiana, Liam knew it was only a matter of time. His brother had been gone off and on for years, but they hadn't seen him for at least two years by then. He knew his mother grieved for Levi, which only fueled Liam's anger toward his twin. The least Levi could do was write home and tell them he was still alive. Their mother had suffered enough with wondering.

Without thinking, Liam began organizing the random tools, but his mind was still stuck on his brother. Truth be known, Liam missed Levi just as much as the rest of the family did, maybe more. But if the family had known where he was, they wouldn't have had to come back to Hollybrook.

At twenty-seven years old, Liam could have easily stayed in Rover's Corner. He could have found a house to rent and gone on with his leather working business. But there wasn't any compelling reason to stay—he wasn't married, so he had no children. Although, one girl in their district had caught his attention. But his parents worked hard to convince him that the family needed to stay together. Liam resisted their pressure until one afternoon, he'd come across his mother crying. She hadn't known he was there or she surely would have tried to pull herself together.

As it was, she sobbed until Liam thought his own heart would break with it. At that moment, he knew he'd have to move to Hollybrook with them. He couldn't let his mother be without both her sons. So, he'd agreed. He'd given his business to his part-time worker Jeff. Jeff had been over the moon, so at least there was that.

Liam walked to the door of the barn and looked out at the large white house standing not too many yards away. He saw movement through one of the windows and knew his mother was arranging things. He looked toward the road and saw his sister Eve walking down the lane.

"Where've you been?" he called out.

"I went to see Rebecca Riehl. I used to call her Becca. You remember her?"

Liam remembered a scrap of a girl with blond hair and blue eyes. She was always with Eve, having no sisters of her own. He remembered that much. He also remembered that she had the sweetest laugh. In truth, it seemed like she was always laughing about something or other. But that was it. He didn't remember anything else. He was a good six or seven years older than her; he'd been much too old to pay her any mind.

"She's got a new *mamm*." Eve walked up to him at the barn door. Her breath was coming out in puffs of white. "Her new *mamm* is hardly older than she is. Name of Amelia. She's got three boys, so Becca's got new brothers, too."

"Oh?"

"*Jah*. You ever heard of her?"

"Amelia? From here?"

"*Nee*. From Linnow Creek." Eve seemed to be digging for information, which was interesting.

"Amelia... What was her last name?"

"No idea." Eve shrugged, looking around. "Where's *Dat?*"

"Out in the fields."

"You gonna work with leather here?"

"Don't rightly know. I hope to. Thought I'd set up a shop in the barn."

"I'm sorry," she said. "You know ... that you had to move with us. Not that I'm not glad. I am. But I know you'd have rather stayed in Rover's Corner."

"And you?"

She shrugged again. "Doesn't make much difference to me. I didn't have a beau, if that's what you're wondering."

Liam scowled. "*Nee.* I wasn't wondering." Eve seemed put out with his answer, but he chose to ignore that. "*Mamm* seems happier. *Dat,* too."

"If only our Levi was here, it'd be perfect."

"Don't get your hopes up. I don't think he is here."

"My hopes are up. One of these days, we'll hear from him. I've been praying, and I know the Lord *Gott* will answer."

"I admire your faith, Eve."

"Don't you have faith? Don't you think we'll see Levi again?"

"I don't rightly know. I hope so, for everyone's sake."

"Liam?"

"Huh?"

"You planning on finding a girl here? Getting hitched?"

Liam frowned at her. He wasn't about to talk of such things with anyone, let alone his sister. Nor was he about to admit that he was lonely at times, and that he yearned for someone special he could call his own. He'd thought there would be a chance of that with Nancy in Rover's Corner, but clearly, that was now out of the question. If it was in God's plan to find someone in Hollybrook, so be it. If not, he'd learn to be content.

"Well?" Eve pressed.

"That's up to *Gott*," he said abruptly and turned to go back inside the barn.

Chapter Eight

Liam had no idea where the people went to get their bridles and harnesses worked on or where they bought new ones. He didn't remember a leather works shop when they'd lived there before. But they'd been gone a long time, and things had changed. He decided to visit around a bit and ask. That was the best way to find out anything.

Since Eve had been so recently at the Riehls' place, he decided to go there first. It was a short distance, which he remembered after he saw his sister return from their place earlier. If he took the cart, he could be there right quick. After the noon meal, he told his parents where he was going and set out.

It didn't take long to arrive. First, he checked the barn for Noah Riehl, but he wasn't there. He did see a young lad of about six or seven running behind the chicken coop as he approached the house. He knew lots of Amish didn't knock when visiting, nor did many use the front door, favoring instead the side door that often led into a wash-up room. But since Liam hadn't been in Hollybrook for years, he decided the front door might be a better choice in his case.

He secured the reins of his horse, jumped out of the cart and climbed the steps. He knocked on the door and waited. Within minutes, it was opened by a young woman with shining blond hair and eyes as clear as the sky on a perfect summer day.

"*Gut* day," he said, staring at her.

She smiled. "*Jah?*"

"I'm Liam Eash."

Her face brightened, and he found himself glad to be standing there with her. "*Ach*, you're Eve's brother. I hardly recognized you."

Well, he certainly wouldn't have recognized her, for this had to be Rebecca Riehl. She had grown into a beautiful young woman. He realized he was gawking at her, but he could hardly help himself. She was about six inches shorter than he was, slender, and with an energy about her that drew him in. He hoped she'd ask him inside.

"Come on in, Liam. How nice to see you again. I'll put on some tea."

"Thank you. Is your *dat* around?" he asked, moving inside. He wanted to follow her into the kitchen while she put on the kettle, but he could hardly do that, now, could he? He hesitated inside the door.

"He's upstairs," she said, and a strange look passed over her face. She straightened her shoulders. "He's usually outside this time of day, but I think he's helping my new stepmother with something."

"I don't mean to bother him. I just had a question or two."

"I'll fetch him. Just let me put the water on first."

She swirled away from him, and he watched the graceful way she moved as she disappeared into the kitchen. Again, he thought about how he'd never paid much mind to Rebecca as a child. She'd just been one of his sister's friends, and he distinctly remembered being frequently annoyed with his sister and any of her friends during those early years. Eve had followed him around like a burr in a dog's paw, so he was only too glad to ignore both her and anyone with her.

A moment later, Rebecca emerged from the kitchen. "*Ach*, Liam, please be seated. I'll just run upstairs now."

In a swirl of motion, she left him and dashed up the stairs. Within minutes, she was back down, her father following her.

"Why, if it ain't Liam Eash," Noah Riehl exclaimed. He put out his thick calloused hand. "How are you, son?"

"I'm right fine," Liam answered, standing again. He could see where Rebecca got her blue eyes.

"What can I do for you?" Noah pulled out the chair at the head of the table. "Sit down. Sit down."

Liam sank back to the side bench. "I worked with leather in Rover's Corner," he started. "Had me a shop. I repaired bridles and such. Even made leather things to sell to the *Englisch*, belts and bags, things like that. I was wondering where you bought your bridles and harnesses 'round here."

"At the Troyer's store, the Feed & Supply. But they don't carry much. Usually have to order things in. And they don't repair."

Liam felt a surge of relief. He nodded. "Well, then, if I was to open a shop, it might do well."

"A shop would be right appreciated as far as I can see."

"And the Troyers?"

"That ain't their main business. They wouldn't be bothered if you was to open a shop of leather goods and repair."

Liam's mind raced. He could get something up and running in the corner of his barn by the end of the week.

"Where you planning to locate?"

"In my barn. Should be handy to most folks."

"Should be."

Rebecca came out of the kitchen carrying a tray with two cups of steaming tea. There was a small plate with cookies on it, too. Liam glanced up at her and noticed that she looked slightly nervous. He wondered why.

"Thank you, daughter," Noah said, reaching for a cup.

Rebecca handed Liam the other, and he found himself wishing he could brush against her hand. How absurd. What was the matter with him that day?

She set the plate of cookies on the table.

"Does Amelia need any help upstairs?" she asked her dad.

"*Nee.* She should be down any minute. She'll be glad to meet you, Liam."

As if his words conjured her up, Liam heard footsteps on the stairs. He looked up to see a woman who looked to be about his age. Her auburn hair was pulled so tightly back into her bun that her eyebrows looked permanently lifted. He was about to open his mouth to say hello when her eyes caught his.

Her mouth twisted open into a grotesque shape, and her face went white. She dropped the glass she was carrying, and it crashed to the steps, shattering and shooting splinters of glass everywhere. She grabbed the railing and looked about to collapse in a heap.

Noah leapt up from his chair and rushed to her, Rebecca right behind him. Liam stood, stunned, wondering what in the world had just happened. The woman seemed to be reacting to him. But why? He'd never seen her before.

"Amelia!" Noah cried, crunching over the glass to grab her arms and keep her from falling. "What is it? What's wrong?"

Rebecca knelt before her on the step right below. "What is it? Are you ill?"

Amelia tore herself from Noah's grip and flapped her hands as if brushing both Noah and Rebecca away. And then she skirted around them, nearly stumbling down the rest of the steps in her haste to get away.

"Amelia!" Noah cried again.

But she was gone. The front door slammed behind her, the loud bang ringing through the house.

"I-I'm sorry," Liam stammered, feeling somehow responsible, but having no idea why. "What can I do?"

Noah looked at him stupidly, as if trying to wrap his mind around what had just occurred. And then, just that quickly, he hustled out the front door in pursuit of his new wife.

Rebecca stood up from the step, clearly shaken. She looked at Liam, bewildered.

"I should go," Liam said, feeling like a complete intruder.

"I-I don't know what happened. Do you think she's ill?" Rebecca asked him.

He didn't think the woman was ill at all. Instead, she seemed completely frightened, as if something had stunned her into a near collapse.

"I don't think so," he told Rebecca, noting how pale she looked, too.

"But what was wrong?" Rebecca's brow lowered even further. "Do you know her?"

"I've never met her before. At least as far as I know. Maybe as a child?"

Rebecca put her hand to her mouth and crossed the room, tiptoeing carefully around the glass and peering out the front window. "I don't see them. I guess whatever it was, *Dat* will take care of it."

"I think I need to be gone when she comes back. In case it was me who set her off." He walked to the door and gazed down at Rebecca. "I'm sorry."

"It wasn't your fault," Rebecca answered. "I hope you got all the information you needed."

"I did. Your *dat* was very helpful." He should leave right away, but he hesitated, wanting to talk with Rebecca further. He wondered if she had a beau. He couldn't imagine why she wouldn't have one, seeing how pretty she was. And nice. He wanted to know more about her.

"I'll be seeing you around then," she said, opening the door.

"*Jah.* I'll be seeing you around," he answered. He walked outside, glancing about, not wanting to intrude upon Noah and his wife again if he could help it. But all seemed perfectly calm out there. He unhitched his pony, climbed into his cart and got underway.

Chapter Nine

Rebecca held onto the edge of the screen door and watched Liam leave. What a nice man. He'd certainly grown taller in the years he'd been gone. Although, she remembered him as tall and skinny from when she was young. But she certainly didn't remember how handsome he was. His blue eyes were startling in their clearness. It was like she could see right inside them. And the golden flecks in his iris shimmered. A shiver ran up her back as she thought about them.

And his smile—so warm and inclusive, like you were the only one he was thinking about. Was he married? No, Eve would have said so, wouldn't she? But how could such a handsome man not be married? Or at least be courting? Had he left a girl in Illinois?

The possibility disturbed her, which was absurd. Why should she care? She'd been with him a whole twenty minutes or so.

She leaned her head against the door for a moment and then

went back inside. She had more serious things to think about. Plus, she needed to sweep up the glass before someone got hurt. The boys could be running in at any time, and they'd shed their shoes in minutes, which would make the mess even more dangerous.

What was wrong with Amelia? Rebecca began to pick up the larger pieces of glass when she remembered Amelia's reaction to Eve. Hadn't that been odd, too? What was it about the Eashes that disturbed Amelia so greatly.

Neither Eve nor Liam knew of ever seeing Amelia before. So, what was it? Rebecca fetched the garbage can and the broom and dustpan. She carefully swept twice over the entire area. She put the garbage can away and then she carried the tea cups to the sink to wash them. Through the window above the sink, she saw her dad leading Amelia back to the house. He had his arm around her waist, but she wasn't leaning into him. In fact, she looked stiff as a thick branch, walking like one of those wind-up toys she'd seen once in an *Englisch* dollar store.

Rebecca stepped back so she wouldn't be seen and studied Amelia's face. It was still white, and her lips were pressed into a thin line. Rebecca didn't know what she should do. Stay where she was, or run to the door and open it for them? The hollow look on Amelia's face told her to stay put, so she did.

The front door opened and shut. It was surprising that her dad would bring Amelia in that way. Or maybe they thought Liam was still there. No, that couldn't be—his pony cart was gone. She heard her father say something, but she couldn't make out what is was. At the same time, the side door slammed, and she knew the boys were back inside. Jumbled, clumping footsteps sounded and then more noise from the front room. Clearly, they hadn't shed their shoes at all.

Rebecca figured her help would be needed. She quickly wiped her hands on the dish towel and went into the front room.

"Boys, your mother needs some quiet. Go on back out and play. There's a tire swing in the tree in front."

"Mamm?" Alex said with his hands on his hips. "What's wrong with you?"

"Nothing's wrong with your *mamm*," Rebecca interjected. "Come on, boys. Want to go outside with me and swing? I can push you up to the sky."

"Mamm?" Alex repeated, clearly wanting an answer.

"Nothing's wrong," Noah said. "She's tired."

"She ain't tired," Michael said, his tone even more sour than usual. "She looks sick."

Amelia opened her mouth, but no sound came. Looking distressed, she closed her mouth in a scowl.

"I don't wanna go outside," young William said, moving closer to his mother.

"Let's go, boys," Rebecca urged. "Last one out is a rotten egg!"

She started to run toward the door, hoping the boys would follow. Running in the house was frowned upon, but she figured these were extenuating circumstances. She didn't get far before the boys started after her. She breathed a sigh of relief and increased her speed out the door. They clattered down the porch steps and into the yard. Rebecca's feet went instantly cold. She didn't have her shoes on, but if she went back into the house, the boys might follow her back inside.

Well, her feet had been cold before, and at least she had her thick socks on.

"Who's first?" she asked, putting on her best and most excited smile.

"Me! Oldest first!" Alex claimed. He wriggled into the tire. "I'm ready."

"Youngest first," William said.

"Don't worry. You'll get your turn right quick," Rebecca said.

"You ain't got shoes on," Michael observed. "It's practically winter, you know."

"I know. I'll get them later."

"Then I'm taking mine off," Williams said. "I don't like shoes."

"*Nee*. Please don't," Rebecca told him. "It's mighty cold. My feet are freezing."

"Then get your shoes," Michael said, his blue eyes drilling into hers.

She sighed. "If I do, will you push your brother till I get back?"

"I don't need no pushing," Alex said, whizzing through the air.

"Then, will you wait here for me?" she asked all of them.

Michael shrugged. "Nothing else to do."

"All right. I'll be back in a jiffy." Rebecca gave them a long look and then ran toward the side door of the house. She only hoped they'd still be there when she got back.

~

Liam spent the afternoon setting up his workspace in the barn. When he was nearly finished, Eve wandered out to join him.

"I had to take a break," she said to him.

"A break from what?"

"*Mamm* is like a tornado in there. I can barely feel my fingers." She stretched out her red, chapped hands and shook her head. "Look. I've almost scrubbed the skin right off."

Liam chuckled. "She's so happy to be back, though."

"That she is." Eve grew quiet for a moment before continuing. "I haven't seen her happy for a long time."

"Since Levi left..."

"*Jah.* Since Levi."

"I think *Dat's* glad to be back, too." Liam stepped away from his array of leather working tools which he had arranged on the wall above the workbench. He gestured to the area. "What do you think?"

"So, you're going to start working with leather here, too?"

"*Jah.* I talked with Noah Riehl and there ain't anyone in the district working with it. Can't get repairs done in town, either."

"That's *gut* for you, then."

"*Jah.* Real *gut.*"

Eve ran her hand lightly over some of the tools. "Maybe you won't be so sad we left Rover's Corner then."

He glanced at her sharply. He hadn't thought his reluctance had been quite so obvious, and this was the second time she'd brought it up. "It'll be okay here."

"Did you meet Noah's new wife?" Eve asked. "She's awful young. Has three boys, too."

Liam was eager to hear what his sister thought of Amelia Riehl.

Eve's expression grew concerned. "There was something strange about her…"

"Oh?"

"When she heard my name, she started acting right odd. And she left the room real quick-like after that. Like she didn't want to visit." Eve gave a slight shrug. "I couldn't understand it."

Liam hesitated, wondering if he should share his experience, too. He decided to go ahead; maybe together, they could figure it out. He hoped it wasn't to be considered gossiping.

He spoke cautiously. "When she saw me, it was like she'd seen a monster. Or a ghost. Her face went white as a duck's feather."

"Really?"

"And she ran away."

Eve's eyes stretched wider. "What was wrong, you think? Is she afraid of strangers? I heard of that once. It's like a disease or something."

Liam shook his head. "I don't think that's it. It's something about us."

"But we don't even know her."

They were silent for a minute, and then, as if on cue, they stared at each other and both of them blurted, "Levi."

"It has to be," Eve said quickly. "My last name. And you... Why, she probably thought you *were* Levi."

"She didn't even stay long enough for introductions. She took one look at me—"

"Which means, she knows Levi! *Ach,* Liam, maybe she knows where he is."

"I guess she never knew Levi had a twin."

"But why wouldn't he tell her that?"

Liam whistled under his breath. "No reason to, I suppose."

"Where do you think he is? Around here, like *Mamm* hopes?"

"Amelia isn't from here. She's from Linnow Creek. At least, I think that's what Rebecca said."

"So, is Levi in Linnow Creek, then? How far is that from here? Shall we go?" Eve was talking fast. "But we better not tell *Mamm* and *Dat.* I don't want them to get their hopes up. *Ach,* Liam. Just think if we could bring Levi home to them."

"You seem to have forgotten something."

She paused. "What?"

"If Levi wanted us to know where he is, he'd tell us. And if we do find him, it's highly likely he isn't going to come home with us."

Eve's face fell. "But surely, he would want to see *Mamm* and *Dat*. Surely, he'd come home with us. At least for a day or two."

Liam sighed. His sister wasn't thinking straight. He knew his brother well enough to know that he wouldn't come home with them. In all likelihood, he wouldn't even want to see them. Otherwise, why was he staying gone? Why hadn't he written? No. His brother was perfectly happy with his disappearance.

"You don't think he'd come," Eve said, deflated.

"*Nee*. I don't think so."

"How does she know him? And it must have been bad, Liam. She was really upset."

"What did he do to her...?" Levi muttered, and seeing the shock on his sister's face, he wished he hadn't spoken out loud. But it was true. It had to have been something awful to cause a reaction like that.

"He wouldn't do anything bad. He wouldn't hurt her." Eve's eyes filled with tears. "Would he?"

"Of course not." Liam took her hand in his and squeezed it before letting go again. "Maybe she fell in love with him or something, and then he left. Or maybe a cousin of hers liked him."

"It couldn't have been Amelia. She was married." Eve frowned. "Although, I don't know how long she's been a widow."

"It's not our business," Liam said, fearing they'd wandered right into gossip. "Nothing *gut* comes from poking our noses in other people's lives."

"But this is our brother we're talking about. I don't care about poking into Amelia's life. Only if she can help us find Levi." Eve drew herself up to her full height and turned to leave.

"Don't do anything stupid," he called after her.

She didn't respond, only kept walking. If he knew Eve, she wouldn't let it rest. At least, not totally. He groaned. This couldn't end well. Amelia was terribly upset, which meant—no matter how he reassured his sister—that Levi had done something horrible. Maybe even unforgivable.

Liam couldn't imagine what, and in truth, he couldn't allow his mind to go there. He turned back to his makeshift shop. He'd have to get word out that he was now open for business. And the best place he knew to get word out, was likely the Feed & Supply.

Chapter Ten

Rebecca snapped the reins on River's rump, and the pony cart gained a bit of speed. She looked behind her to where her three new brothers were sitting in the back, huddled together, looking mighty sullen. She'd been happy to leave the farm to go to the Feed & Supply for a fifty-pound bag of flour. And she hadn't even minded taking the boys.

Giving Amelia more time to settle down was fine with her. But the boys weren't any too pleased. She glanced at them again.

"Anybody here like licorice?" she asked.

Alex perked up. "What kind? The black kind or the red kind?"

"Either one."

"I like red," William said.

"Me, too," Alex agreed. He pointed to Michael, who hadn't said anything. "He likes the black kind."

"How about we get some of both?" she asked, knowing full well that she was trying to bribe them into being more pleasant, and maybe even liking her.

"*Jah!*" William said, grinning now.

Michael shrugged, but Rebecca thought she saw the smallest twinge of a smile on his face.

"We're almost there," she told them and gave another snap to the reins.

The lot of the Feed & Supply had two carts and three buggies in it. Rebecca saw that one of them was Naomi King's who ran a nearby Bed and Breakfast. Rebecca hadn't seen her in a while, since she'd missed the last church Sunday. As soon as she got the cart stopped, the boys hurdled out of the back. They ran ahead of her into the store; although, she noted that Alex was basically pulling Michael along.

She secured her pony and started toward the steps into the store herself. Before she got there, the door opened and Liam stepped out. She gave a start, not expecting to see him again so soon. Her pulse quickened and she found herself pleased, which caused her cheeks to go warm.

He came down the steps and stopped before her. "Why, hello again, Rebecca."

"Hello," she said, feeling suddenly tongue-tied.

He looked over her shoulder to where she'd parked her cart. "That yours?"

She nodded.

"And the boys who just went running into the store? Your new brothers?" He smiled at her as if they shared a secret.

She nodded. "*Jah*. My new brothers."

"They look mighty excited about something."

"I promised them licorice."

His brow rose and then he started laughing. "I see how it is. They didn't want to come with you, did they?"

She shrugged, smiling now. "Not really."

He turned serious. "How's your stepmother?"

She chewed the corner of her lip. "Better, I think."

"I hope so—"

"I'm sorry you had to witness that. I know she was embarrassed."

"I won't spread tales, if she's worried."

"*Ach*, I never thought you would." She gazed at him, appreciating his sensitivity. "But thank you."

He raised a shoulder. "You're welcome."

Not able to think of anything else to say, she made to go around him, but he shifted slightly, cutting her off.

"Rebecca?"

She was struck again by the depth of his blue eyes, by the way he looked at her—as if seeing her very thoughts. "*Jah?*"

"I spoke with Eve." He glanced around, and they were still alone. "She told me how Amelia seemed flustered by our last name."

Rebecca nodded, feeling uncomfortable. She didn't think it was appropriate to be discussing Amelia like this. She needed to have loyalty for this woman who had come into her life so abruptly.

"We think we know why."

Rebecca's thoughts of loyalty flew out of her head. "Why?" she asked, unconsciously moving closer to him.

"Levi."

Rebecca frowned, not understanding. "Your brother?"

"My *twin* brother. We think she somehow knew Levi. When she saw me, she might have thought *I* was Levi."

Rebecca covered her mouth with her hand. This made sense. Perfect sense. "Oh, my," she said softly through her fingers.

"We might be wrong, of course. But it would explain things."

"It would," she had to agree.

"Anyway, I wanted to share that. It ain't any of our business, of course, but there it is."

She nodded slowly. "Thank you." She took a deep breath. "Thank you for telling me."

He smiled at her and touched the sleeve of her dress before dropping his hand. "I thought you should know."

"*Jah.*"

"I'll be seeing you, then. *Gut* day, Rebecca."

And just like that, he switched from speaking in an almost intimate manner to speaking to her as if she were the district's schoolmarm. "*Gut* day," she murmured in reply, as he took his leave.

She turned toward the steps, her mind whirling. He had to be right. If Amelia knew Levi, it would explain her reaction. She faltered. But only if something awful had happened between them. Something that had scared Amelia—or upset her very, very badly. What could it have been?

Rebecca figured that Amelia and Levi would be about the same age. Had Levi gone to Linnow Creek when he'd run away? Had he done something to Amelia? A shudder went up Rebecca's spine. This kind of thinking was most unpleasant. She didn't want to stand there guessing what horrible thing had happened. Besides, she didn't even know if it was true. It was all conjecture, after all.

She reached the top step and pulled open the door to the tinkling of a bell. She headed straight for the candy aisle, and not surprisingly, she found her three new brothers leaning over the licorice, nearly drooling with anticipation.

Chapter Eleven

The next few days were busy as Rebecca and her new family maneuvered around each other, trying to build a new normal. Rebecca found herself deferring to Amelia many times a day— sometimes, even many times an hour. Clearly, Amelia was back to herself, establishing new routines in the kitchen and with the chores. Rebecca felt out of place and out of sorts as she tried her hardest not to get in the way, while still being helpful. It was an uncomfortable and unpredictable situation.

"I'll start laundry later in the morning," Amelia announced on the Monday after a no-church Sunday. "First, I'll make the week's cookies."

Rebecca bit her lip to keep from arguing. Whoever heard of not starting the laundry first thing in the morning? Otherwise, how could a person be sure to finish before supper? Even when it was just she and her father, Rebecca had done the laundry first thing. If the air was damp, the clothes took a long time to dry hanging outside—even after being hand-fed through the tight wringer. Since it was only November, they still used the clothesline every week. Unless it was raining of course. And that Monday, it wasn't raining at all.

"I could start it for you," Rebecca finally offered. With six in the house now, they'd have to do multiple loads.

Amelia pursed her lips, and her brows tightened over her eyes. "Fine," she said, her voice thin. "If you insist..."

Rebecca backtracked quickly. "*Nee*. It's all right. I can wait. Do you want help with the baking?"

"I don't need no help." Amelia sighed, clearly rethinking her words. "I mean, it would be right nice to have you start the laundry."

"I'll get to it," Rebecca said. She turned to go down to the basement. She wanted so badly to ask Amelia if everything was all right now. She wanted to know if she'd gotten over whatever it was that had upset her so deeply. And Rebecca was curious if it truly had been about Levi Eash. She looked back at Amelia, who hadn't seemed to notice her hesitation.

"Amelia?" she ventured.

"*Jah?*" Amelia didn't look up from gathering her baking supplies.

"I was wondering if I could invite Eve Eash over to share a meal sometime."

When Rebecca saw Amelia visibly tense, she felt guilty. What was she playing at? She wasn't an *Englisch* spy or something. This wasn't her business.

"Never mind," she said quickly.

Amelia looked at her. Again, she'd turned pale. Rebecca licked her lips nervously.

"Never mind," she repeated.

Amelia's eyes narrowed, and Rebecca had the horrifying realization that Amelia knew full-well what she was doing. Rebecca took a step back, feeling truly terrible now. There was no sound in the kitchen except the soft ticking of the battery clock over the window. Rebecca didn't know what to do. She'd gone too far, and she knew it.

"Do what you want," Amelia finally said, her voice both harsh and resigned. "It's only a matter of time, anyway."

Rebecca didn't understand her last comment, but she wasn't about to continue standing there like a curious cat, waiting to pounce again. She'd done enough. She drew in a breath and tried to smile before escaping down the basement steps.

Standing in the dank basement, she didn't light a lantern right away. If the clouds outside would clear, more light would come in through the tiny windows at the top of each wall. The hulking gas washer, with its large tub and the wringer perched above it, stood next to the far wall, where the spigot was located. A clothesline was strung close to the ceiling for use in the deepest winter or on rainy days.

Rebecca closed her eyes. What secret did Amelia have? What burden was she carrying? And did her father know about it? Had Amelia confided in him?

Disgusted with herself for her unending questions, Rebecca shook her head. She reached for the lantern that was always left on the long shelf. The matches were right beside it, and she struck one and lit the wick. Light permeated the space. Baskets of dirty laundry were waiting in the middle of the floor.

She'd better get started.

~

Rebecca drove her pony cart to the Eash's farm that Sunday evening. She had turned down Eve's offer to come and pick her up, not wanting the possibility of Amelia being confronted with Eve again. Besides, she enjoyed driving River. In truth, River was like a friend to her—always eager to see her and always cooperative when hitched. Her dad scoffed at Rebecca's feelings for the pony, for he saw his animals primarily for the service they could provide. But not Rebecca. She loved the pony and took her treats of carrots and apples regularly.

At age twenty, Rebecca should have a beau. Some of her friends were already married, and most of those who weren't, were secretly seeing boys. Try as she might, Rebecca wasn't really interested in anyone in their district. For months, she had been looking forward to a shared youth event—when other districts would join them for games and activities. That didn't happen often; it was too unhandy to secure transportation for some of the groups that came from Ohio. But when it worked out, it was wonderful. Everyone was able to extend their friendship circle.

And it was the perfect opportunity to meet potential beaus.

Rebecca clucked her tongue at River and turned onto the Eash property. She found herself not thinking of Eve, however. Her thoughts were on Liam. Now, there was a man she admired. She still didn't know if he was attached, and she was embarrassed to ask

Eve outright. In truth, Eve might not even know, as such things were kept secret. Rebecca hoped Liam didn't have anyone special in his life. She hoped that maybe he'd want to get to know her better. She hoped...

Her breath caught. Both Eve and Liam were on the front porch. Was he going with them? She pulled up to the porch.

"Hi, Becca!" Eve called, bounding down the steps. "I hope you don't mind, but I talked Liam into coming."

Did this mean he didn't have a girlfriend back in Rover's Corner? Rebecca's pulse quickened, and she smiled at Eve.

"*Nee.* It's fine."

Liam came down the steps, his eyes steady on her. "May I drive?" he asked, his rich voice rumbling over her.

She blinked. "Uh, *jah.* Certainly."

She scooted over on the bench, and after he climbed in, she handed him the reins. The cart dipped with his weight as he sat beside her. Eve had climbed into the back of the cart and was balancing on an upside-down wooden box they kept there for extra seating. Rebecca didn't know what to do. Should she go back there with Eve? It didn't seem right that she should sit next to Liam as he drove.

Before she could come to a decision, however, Liam snapped the reins and they were off.

"How are you, Rebecca?" he asked.

"I'm fine," she answered, trying wildly to think of something clever and witty to say, but her tongue seemed to be glued in place and nothing came to mind.

"Liam's opened his leather shop again," Eve offered from behind.

Rebecca let out her breath. "Have you?" she asked him.

"*Jah*. In the barn. Soon I hope to lease someplace more central to folks in the district. Or build a small shop on the property. But for right now, the barn should suit."

"He did real *gut* in Rover's Creek," Eve said.

Rebecca saw Liam's cheeks color at her compliment.

"How nice," she said, and then cringed. She was proving herself to be completely inept at conversation.

"Do they always have singings on church Sundays?" Liam asked.

"Most times, they do. Lots of people come." Rebecca glanced back at Eve who looked mighty pleased by the news. Rebecca imagined that Eve was eager to meet some eligible bachelors. She thought of Corey Peachey. He was nice and as far as Rebecca knew, he wasn't courting anyone. She'd be sure to point him out to Eve.

Liam handled the cart with ease, as if River was his pony and he'd driven her many times. Liam's hands were large and strong-looking, calloused from work. She wondered if his skin would be rough. Her eyes widened. Land's sakes, the way her thoughts ran away with her these days—especially where Liam was concerned.

Every girl at the singing was going to notice him, of that she had no doubt. If they saw her arrive with him, they would shower her with questions. Or maybe, they'd think he was courting her. After all, she was on the bench beside him. Maybe sitting there had been a good idea, after all. She wasn't eager to have other girls hoping to capture his attention.

"Don't you think?" Eve was saying.

Rebecca gave a start. Had Eve asked her something? She had no idea what they were even talking about.

"Rebecca?" Eve asked.

"I'm sorry, what were you asking?"

"Never mind. We're here, aren't we?"

"We're here," Liam said, adding their cart to the long row of buggies.

Rebecca saw quite a number of courting buggies, all enclosed to keep the occupants out of the public eye. She suddenly wished that she were in a courting buggy with Liam—

"Will you introduce me?" Eve asked, climbing out. "Some people I remember from before, but there were a lot of folks at church this morning I didn't recognize."

"I'll be happy to," Rebecca said, scrambling down quickly.

Liam was already unhitching the pony so she could graze during the meeting.

"Come on," Eve said, pulling Rebecca's arm.

They walked into the barn, which was already teeming with youth of all ages, some quite young and others well into their twenties. As long as you were single, you were welcomed into the group; although, at times, married folks stopped in to keep an eye on things. Rebecca spotted Rueben Yoder, holding a songbook with slips of paper sticking out from the pages. He looked ready to begin.

The Yoders had set the tables end-to-end, so that they formed one long table. The boys sat on one side and the girls on the other. Not every family did it that way. Sometimes, they sat around in clusters to sing—the boys and girls always separated, of course. She and Eve slipped onto the bench on the girls' side. She watched the door, waiting for Liam to come in. There was space directly across from her, and she hoped that was where he'd sit.

But he didn't. He came into the barn and sat at the bench on the opposite end of the tables. Now there was no way she could watch him or even see him without craning her head—and she wasn't about to do that.

As soon as he sat down, the whispered buzzing on her side of the table increased—just as she knew it would. Everyone was noticing the handsome newcomer to the group. She saw Josie Studer practically preening when she caught sight of him. Rebecca inwardly groaned. Josie was one of the prettiest girls in the district with her wide hazel eyes and button nose. Rebecca reached up to pat her hair below her *kapp,* glad that it still felt tight and orderly, but knowing she couldn't compete with Josie's beauty.

"Who's that?" Eve whispered to her, motioning with her head toward none other than Corey Peachy.

Rebecca almost laughed out loud. She'd been right about the possible match. "Corey Peachey," she whispered back. "He's right nice."

Eve flushed with pleasure and folded her hands on her lap.

"Don't fret," Rebecca continued. "I'll make sure you're introduced."

Eve shook her head. "*Nee. Nee.* It'll be too forward."

"Weren't you just asking me to introduce you around?"

"I changed my mind." Eve clamped her lips closed, but her cheeks remained flushed.

"Suit yourself," Rebecca said, but she still planned to introduce them.

Chapter Twelve

Rueben stood at the head of the long row of tables and held up his hands. "*Gut* evening, friends. Is everybody ready to sing to the Lord *Gott* tonight?"

Everyone murmured their assent, and he opened the event with silent prayer and then got right to the singing. Rebecca joined in heartily, loving the harmony of everyone's voices. To her, it sounded like what the angels must sound like in heaven. Everyone there had a lot of practice singing, as they had sung every day together during their eight years of schooling. She thought that the youth sounded even better than when all the people sang at church service.

Eve had a sweet voice, and she sang out with real enthusiasm. Rebecca noticed that Eve's gaze darted regularly toward Corey, and if she wasn't mistaken, Corey was quite aware of Eve.

After the last song was sung, refreshments were served, and sure enough, there was a big tub of ice cream.

"Just made it yesterday, you know," Rueben announced. Rebecca well remembered when the Yoders purchased a gas freezer. All the youth had been excited, anticipating lots of ice cream.

It didn't take everyone long to jump up from the benches and head over to the food table. Rueben's mother had come out to join them and was serving up the ice cream. Rebecca maneuvered herself and Eve over to where Corey was waiting with his bowl. When Eve realized what Rebecca was doing, she made a move to leave, but Rebecca had her hemmed in.

"Hi Corey," she said casually.

"Well hello, Rebecca."

"I don't know if you remember Eve Eash? Her family used to live here a while back."

Corey's brow rose. "That's who you are," he blurted. "I knew you looked familiar. You weren't at service this morning, were you?"

Eve nodded.

"I didn't see you. Well, that could have been because I was right in front, and then I was watching my nephew during the meal time. He talks my ears off, that one."

Eve smiled. "Nice to meet you again, Corey." Her voice was nearly breathless.

Rebecca grinned and hung back just a little—but not so much as to be too noticeable. She wanted to give Eve every chance to speak to Corey without her. Corey was a talker, so Eve didn't have to say much. Rebecca kept backing up as subtly as she could.

She bumped into someone and turned around, her knees going a bit weak at the sight of Liam.

"You aren't eating?" Liam asked, gazing at the empty plate in her hand.

She smiled. "Sorry for knocking into you. And I just haven't gotten anything yet."

His smile was warm. "The ice cream looks *gut*."

"It will be. The Yoders make the best."

Liam nodded and walked to where a group had gathered around the tub of ice cream, leaving her staring after him. Rebecca ended up chatting with a few of her friends, but mainly she remained quiet, listening to them speculate about who was courting whom. She had never given that too much attention. Oh, of course, she thought about courting now and again. When she was seventeen, she remembered pondering possible beaus quite a bit. But not lately.

Strangely, she now found herself yearning for a beau. It would be nice to have a special someone in her life. She thought of her father and how he seemed so much happier now that he had Amelia. She often caught him smiling for no reason she could see. And usually, her father wasn't much of a smiler.

Falling in love again had done that to him.

Falling in love. She touched her fingers to her lips and wondered what it felt like. Was it anything like the tingles she experienced when she looked into Liam's eyes?

"Becca?"

Rebecca looked at Eve who had just joined her. "Hi, Eve. Did you get any treats?"

Eve nodded. Her face was flushed, and her eyes twinkled. She picked up a thick chocolate chip cookie and took a bite. Rebecca introduced her to everyone, and most of them either remembered Eve or had heard that the Eashes were back.

After another hour or so, everyone began to wander out to their buggies to go home. Liam came over to them and said that he'd hitch up River and they could be on their way.

"All right, Liam," Eve replied, but she wasn't really looking at him. Her eyes were wandering, and Rebecca figured she was trying to spot Corey.

"You like him, don't you?" Rebecca said softly, close to Eve's ear.

Eve immediately turned bright red. "I don't know what you're talking about," she countered.

"Right." Rebecca laughed. "You have no idea."

"Let's go outside to wait for Liam," Eve suggested, obviously wanting to change the subject.

"Okay."

"And can you come by tomorrow? I want to ask you something."

Rebecca gave her a quizzical look. "All right."

Liam pulled up in the cart and the girls climbed in. Rebecca hesitated where to sit, but Eve solved that for her.

"You sit in front, Becca," she said. "You're gonna have to drive home from our farm anyway."

Rebecca was pleased, even though she was careful to keep her face neutral. She sat beside Liam. He looked back over his shoulder. "You ready, Eve?"

"Ready."

He snapped the reins and they were on their way, having to wait a bit at the road for two buggies in front of them. The ride home was cold. Rebecca shivered and huddled down further inside her woolen cape. She wished she'd brought her black outer bonnet to put over her *kapp*. Her ears were freezing. Liam was quiet on the way to the Eash farm. Even Eve didn't say much, which Rebecca found odd. Perhaps, she was dreaming about Corey. Rebecca grinned at the thought.

"Something funny?" Liam asked, smiling at her.

Had he been watching her? She blinked. "*Nee*, not really." Her cheeks warmed, and she searched for something else to say, but absolutely nothing came to mind—except how handsome he was and how nice it felt to be sitting beside him. Which of course, she wouldn't dare utter.

Eve piped up from behind. "You'll remember to come tomorrow, won't you?"

"I'll remember," Rebecca said.

In the thin light of the lantern that Liam had hung from the front corner of the cart, Rebecca could see his brow rise. Eve said no more, and Rebecca wondered again what it was all about.

"Here we are," Liam said. He waited for Eve to get out, but he didn't move.

"Ain't you coming?" Eve asked.

"I'm going to drive Rebecca home."

Rebecca's gaze flew to him. He *was?*

"What are you going to do with her pony cart then when you come back here?" Eve asked.

"I'm walking home from her house."

"You don't have to do that," Rebecca said, although she couldn't have been happier at the idea. She liked this thoughtful man. She liked him a lot.

"But I do have to," he said. "I can't have you driving home alone in the dark."

"See you tomorrow, then," Eve said, holding up her hand in a wave. "Bye, Becca."

"Bye, Eve."

Liam clicked his tongue, and River pulled the cart away from the porch.

"You really don't have to drive me home," Rebecca said again.

He was silent for a moment, and then he turned to her. "Rebecca, it wouldn't be right."

His voice was soft, and in the quiet darkness of the night, his words sounded intimate, as if he had planned this drive from the beginning with the sole purpose of courting her. She sucked in a quiet breath at her thoughts. She was imagining things, for sure and for certain.

But how she wished he was thinking of her romantically. At least a little. As the cart rolled over the asphalt, rocking in a gentle rhythm, she allowed herself to dream. Allowed herself to pretend that he *was* courting her. Her heart warmed, and she realized again how much she yearned for someone in her life to call her own. She glanced at him out of the corner of her eye. His profile was strong and solid, and she felt so completely safe by his side. And not only safe—but special and treasured.

She swallowed. She was getting out of control, but she couldn't help herself. She clasped her hands tightly in her lap.

"Are you cold?" he asked.

"Not really," she answered. "Well, maybe a little."

He reached over and put his hand over hers. She flinched—not because she didn't want his hand there, but because she was so stunned that he would do such a thing. He pulled back just as quickly, and she got the feeling that he was as surprised by his gesture as she was. But the warmth of his hand, the feel of his fingers on hers, remained.

"Sorry," he mumbled and looked straight ahead. He clicked his tongue again, and River sped up.

Liam pulled the cart into her drive, and she found herself wishing he would have kept going. Maybe gone at least as far as the King's Bed and Breakfast before turning around and taking her home. But it was too late for that. He was already pulling up to her porch.

"I'll need to see to the cart and River," she said.

"No need. I'll see to them. You get in out of the cold."

She looked at him, and in the lantern light, his eyes looked nearly black. "You don't have to do that."

"Rebecca," he said, and his voice was both patient and tender, "will you allow me to take care of things for you?"

Tingles went up and down her spine as she kept her eyes on him. Her mouth went dry as sudden fierce affection for him swept through her.

"A-all right," she said.

"Rebecca?"

"*Jah?*"

"Maybe, I can take you home after the next singing, too."

Her breath caught. Did his offer mean more than a ride home? Did it mean that he *was* interested in her and wanted to get to know her better? Perhaps court her? Her body trembled with anticipation. She could scarcely believe it was happening.

"*J-jah,*" she stammered. "*Jah.* I'd like that."

He grinned widely. "All right then."

"Thank you, Liam."

"You're welcome, Rebecca."

She slid down from the cart and watched as he circled the drive and headed for the barn. She hugged herself tightly, and then she went into the house.

She couldn't stop smiling.

Chapter Thirteen

"Amelia, I'm going to run over to a friend's house, if that's all right," Rebecca said. Her goats had been tended, and she had already put on a roast for the noon meal. She avoided telling Amelia which friend she was going to see. Amelia had been acting normally of late, and Rebecca feared causing another reaction.

Amelia looked up from her mending. "How long will you be gone?"

"I don't rightly know. Shouldn't be long. Do you need something?" Rebecca wasn't used to asking permission, so to speak. When it was just she and her dad, she set her own schedule, and as long as the household ran smoothly, he didn't pay much mind to her doings.

Amelia seemed to consider her question. "*Nee.* I'm fine. The boys will be hungry when they get home from school."

Rebecca's brow crinkled, unsure why Amelia was telling her that. The boys wouldn't be home for hours.

"Go on with you," Amelia finally said, concentrating again on her needle and thread.

Rebecca went to the wash room and grabbed her cape. She put on her heavy black shoes and laced them tightly. She wound a scarf around her neck and stepped through the side door, closing it behind her. The air outside was cool, although not as cold as the night before. She hurried across the yard and out to the road. There didn't seem to be anyone about. An occasional car zoomed past her, but other than that, no one. When she reached the Eash farm, she couldn't help but look about for Liam.

But then, he'd be in the barn, wouldn't he? Wasn't that where he was setting up his shop? She would love to see his work. She imagined the craftsmanship was fine. How could it not be, if Liam was doing it? She snickered under her breath. She had it bad.

Before she even got to the house, Eve ran outside to meet her.

"You came!"

"I told you I would."

"Come on with me to my room."

"Your room?"

"I want to talk private-like."

Her curiosity rising even higher, Rebecca followed her inside. She greeted Olivia Eash in the kitchen before heading up the stairs. Eve was careful to close her door before coming back and flouncing on her bed.

"Sit with me," she instructed.

Rebecca sat.

"Would you like to go to Linnow Creek with me?" she asked, her light blue eyes turning dark with intensity.

"Linnow Creek? Why?"

"I'm going to visit my third cousin."

"Oh? Why?"

A strange look crossed Eve's face, but it was immediately covered with a somewhat forced-looking smile. "I haven't seen her in ages and ages. Not since we left Hollybrook all those years ago."

"Any reason why you're going so soon after just getting here?" There was something more to this request, that was plain.

"I don't know." Eve shrugged. "I want to reconnect. See her again. She's family."

"That she is. It seems odd that I'd go with you. Why not go with your *mamm*?"

Eve shrugged again. "I thought you might enjoy getting away for a day or two. You know, given how things have been for you."

Rebecca pondered the idea. She hadn't said a whole lot about how things had been at home for her. She hadn't shared the true level of tension she felt being in the changed household, or how hard she was trying to find her way. But the idea of getting away did appeal. Eve was right about that.

"Two days?"

"*Jah.*"

"But my goats..."

"Can't someone milk them for you?"

Rebecca bit her lip. She had been teaching Alex how to do it, but she'd never left him on his own. Maybe if her dad could help him a little.

Eve put her hand on Rebecca's knee. "I can see it in your eyes. You want to go, don't you?"

"We'd have to hire a van."

"*Jah.*"

"It'll cost money."

Eve nodded. "I know. I'd pay, of course. It's my idea and my cousin. And I'd make all the arrangements."

Rebecca considered. "It does sound nice."

"So, you'll come?" Eve gushed. "Really?"

"I'll ask my *dat*. And talk to Amelia."

Eve clapped, and then stopped abruptly, looking toward her door. "I'll make arrangements with a driver. Tomorrow, then? We can come by around nine."

"That would give me time to milk the goats before I go, which would mean that Alex would only have to do it that evening and the next day." Rebecca grinned, now caught up in the entire plan. "I'll go home right away and ask. If I can't go, I'll come back to tell you. But if I can go, just pick me up tomorrow."

Eve looked positively jittery as she gave Rebecca a quick hug. "Thank you, Becca. Thank you."

Rebecca laughed. "You're welcome."

"I'll take you back down," she said.

"Maybe I'll stop for a few minutes and visit with your *mamm*."

"*Nee*," Eve blurted. "I mean, uh, she's so busy. She don't like to be disturbed sometimes."

Rebecca frowned. Who didn't like a quick break to visit for a spell, but she didn't argue with Eve. She had to figure out the best way to ask her dad so he'd agree. They went back down the stairs and outside.

"I'll see you tomorrow. We'll be there about nine."

Rebecca nodded. "Tomorrow."

Eve made an odd squeaking noise that Rebecca could only interpret as excitement before she rushed back inside. Rebecca walked toward the road, slowing slightly as she went by the barn. How she wanted to go inside and see if Liam were there, but that would hardly be fitting. She inwardly moaned about her lost opportunity when Liam appeared in the barn door. He leaned against the wooden frame and gave her a slow smile.

Had her thoughts conjured him up? She didn't care. All she knew was that he was there, watching her, smiling, and looking so wonderful it nearly brought tears to her eyes. Her mouth went dry just as it had the night before.

"*Gut* morning, Rebecca," he said, his rich, deep voice reaching her in waves.

"Morning," she answered. She paused for a moment, and they grinned at each other. Then, realizing she must look a fool gaping at him, she nodded and continued on her way to the road.

She was doing a whole lot of smiling lately.

Chapter Fourteen

Rebecca waited until supper to broach the subject of her trip the next morning. She knew she was pushing it with the time limit, but for some reason she was hesitant to bring it up earlier. In truth, she had a niggling feeling that something was a bit off with Eve's invitation. But Eve was her friend, and she decided to have confidence in her.

Supper had been boisterous, with the boys teasing each other, and even knocking into each other amidst giggles and complaints. Rebecca was stunned that her father put up with it. She remembered very quiet, calm meals when she was a child—there was no silliness tolerated. She wondered if her father was indulging them because things were still fairly new.

"I would like to ask something," she said abruptly.

Her dad turned to her. "What is it, daughter?"

"Eve is going to Linnow Creek tomorrow to visit her third cousin. She wants me to accompany her."

"Tomorrow?" Amelia blurted. "Linnow Creek?" Her face went stiff. Rebecca held her breath, praying Amelia wouldn't lose it again. But she didn't. She visibly composed herself and put on a bland expression.

"Awful short notice, *ain't so?*" her father asked.

"*Jah*, it is. I'm sorry about that. I think Eve just decided spur of the minute."

"And your goats?"

"I can milk them and feed them in the morning. I've been teaching Alex to tend them. I think he could do it, if you just watch over him."

Alex gawked at her. "Really? You'd let me do it by myself?"

She gave him an affectionate smile. "You think you're ready?"

"Sure, I am." He looked at her father. "Can I, Noah? I know what to do. Honest."

Her father chuckled and leaned over, stretching out his arm to tousle Alex's hair. "I reckon you're ready for some more responsibility around here."

"What about me?" William piped up.

Alex gave him a tolerant look. "I s'pose you could help."

Rebecca licked her top lip and waited for her dad's edict.

"Go on, then, Rebecca. Have yourself a *gut* time. I'll give you a bit of money."

Rebecca lit up. "Thanks, *Dat.* I'll be leaving around nine." She glanced at Amelia who was quite busy studying her food.

"I get to do the goats by myself," Alex said, his expression smug. He looked at Rebecca. "Thanks, Becca."

She gave a start. How did he know her nickname? Only Eve used it. Maybe he'd known another Rebecca with that nickname back in Linnow Creek. But the fact that he did know it, and that he used it, pleased her immensely.

~

After *redding* up the kitchen for breakfast the next morning, and after listening to her father's nightly Bible reading, Rebecca excused herself to her room. It didn't take her long to pack. After all, they weren't staying but one night. When she had set her small suitcase next to her door, she sat on her bed and let her thoughts wander to Liam.

What was he doing about then? Was he out in the barn, working by lantern light? Or was he listening to his dad read the Bible?

Was he thinking of her?

She pressed her hand gently against her throat and closed her eyes. She saw again the way he looked at her in the darkness after the singing. She heard again his words, saying that he wanted to give her a ride home again. Oh, she liked him. She liked him so much. Were they going to become sweethearts?

She hoped so. With all her heart, she hoped so. She sat there for the longest time, just dreaming of him.

～

Rebecca stood on the front porch in the cold, her suitcase at her feet. The van should be there any minute. She was excited. She hadn't gone anywhere for an awful long time. She found it ironic, and slightly troublesome, that her father had given her permission to go to Linnow Creek with Eve, when he had discouraged her from going to his own wedding there. It still pained her.

But it was a different day, and she was going on an adventure of sorts. She wasn't going to let anything discourage her. There was a crunch on the drive and she looked up to see the van coming. It pulled to a stop at the steps. She'd already said good-bye to everyone, so she picked up her bag and flew down the stairs.

Eve already had the door open to the backseat.

"Morning, Becca," she said.

"Morning."

Rebecca greeted the driver and within minutes, they were underway. Eve leaned close to her. "I have something for you."

"You do?" Rebecca couldn't imagine what.

Eve slipped a folded piece of paper into her hands. "I didn't read it. I promise."

"But what is it?"

"It's from Liam."

Rebecca gasped. "Liam?"

Eve nodded, looking mighty pleased. "Truth be told, I can't believe he gave it to me to give to you. I guess he really wanted you to have it right away. Otherwise, he would have mailed it."

Rebecca pressed it to her chest, her heart thrumming wildly.

"Go on and read it," Eve said. "I'll look out the window for a while." And she did just that, making a huge show of turning away to give Rebecca her privacy. Rebecca hesitated. She felt more inclined to wait and cherish Liam's words when she was alone, but she just couldn't wait. She unfolded his letter and began reading.

Dear Rebecca,

I hope this finds you well this morning. I was thinking about you in the night and found I couldn't wait to talk to you again. So, I'm writing. It's not the same as talking in person, but a close second.

Thank you for inviting Eve on your trip today. She is most excited about going. I hope your cousin in Linnow Creek is doing better—

Rebecca pressed the letter to her chest and stared at Eve. What had her friend done?

"Why does Liam think we're visiting *my* cousin, not yours?" she asked. She saw Eve tense. "Eve? Please turn around."

Slowly, Eve turned to face her. Her eyes were huge and guilt was written all over her face.

"What have you done?"

"I'm so sorry, Becca. Truly, I am. I didn't know what else to do." She shook her head over and over.

"What do you mean?"

"I *have* to go to Linnow Creek. I *have* to. I think my brother Levi might be there. I have to find him."

Rebecca's forehead creased. "But Eve, why lie about it?"

"I couldn't let my *mamm* get her hopes up. She's waited so long to find Levi. I thought if I could find him, I could convince him to come home. To put *Mamm's* heart at rest. She frets so."

Rebecca let out her breath in a long sigh. She had known something was up. Eve's invitation the day before hadn't felt right. Hadn't Rebecca suspected it was something more than a mere visit to Eve's cousin? But *this?* Rebecca shook her head.

Still... As much as she hated what Eve was doing, she understood. She truly did. Didn't she have her own missing brother? She'd give the moon to have Amos back.

But there was no overlooking the deceit.

"It's wrong," she said. "I've lied to my family now."

"No, you haven't," Eve was quick to reassure her. "We *will* stay with my third cousin. She just doesn't know it yet."

"So, you told no one the truth." Rebecca smoothed out Liam's letter and turned it upside down on her lap so Eve couldn't read it.

"Just you. Right now." Eve grabbed her arm. "Please, Rebecca. Please let me do this. Please don't make the driver go back. You didn't lie."

Rebecca bit the inside of her lip. She supposed Eve was right—she hadn't lied. But still, the whole trip was a lie.

"If it was your brother..." Eve let her voice fade.

Rebecca inhaled sharply. "I would do the same thing." She put her hand to her mouth. "I would do the same thing."

"It's just that after your stepmother's reaction, I thought Levi could be in Linnow Creek. It makes sense, don't you think?"

Rebecca nodded. It did make sense.

"And if I don't find him, we'll have our visit with Deborah and then go home."

"But I don't have a cousin in Linnow Creek. You told your family—"

"I know. I know. I'm going to have to confess. But if I find Levi, they'll forgive me. I know they will."

"And if you don't?"

"Then I'll take my punishment."

Rebecca looked at Eve's face and saw the hope there. The very same hope she held in her heart for her own brother. How odd that they both grieved for missing brothers.

"All right, Eve. But I won't be lying for you."

"I know, Becca. Thank you."

Eve sank back into the seat. "But just think... Maybe I'll be seeing my brother soon."

Rebecca hoped it was true, but her practical nature told her it wasn't. Poor Eve. Her heart was set on it. So set, in fact, that she was willing to deceive her own family.

"Becca?"

"Jah?"

"Is Liam sweet on you?"

Rebecca felt her cheeks go hot and knew she was blushing.

"It's all right if he is," Eve rushed on. "In truth, I hope he is."

Rebecca didn't answer.

"You don't have to say anything," Eve went on. "I know our ways. I'm going to look out the window again, though. You know, to give you some more privacy."

Rebecca grinned. She should be angry with Eve, but she wasn't. She didn't see how anyone could be angry at Eve—at least, not for long.

She picked up Liam's letter and continued reading.

There's not really much to say. I'm eager to hopefully get some business this week. Zebadiah, whose farm is to the south, already brought some well-worn bridles in for repair.

I'll close now. I just wanted to tell you that I'm looking forward to the next singing. This time, we'll take my buggy. And I'll find Eve another way to get home.

Yours truly,

Liam

Rebecca smiled. How was it that she had come so quickly to this place? To this place of being smitten; to this place of eagerness for what the future held; to this place of hope for true love?

She glanced at the back of Eve's head and smiled. It was nice to be together again. Nice to have her friend back from Illinois. Whatever was set to happen in Linnow Creek, Rebecca was glad she could be there for Eve. Glad they would be together.

There had been so much change and so fast. Things weren't perfect —she knew that. And in truth, they didn't have to be. But they were good. And the days ahead were ripe for happiness.

She sighed and leaned back against the vinyl seat, then she folded Liam's letter and carefully tucked it away in the bodice of her dress.

The End

Continue Reading...

✾

Thank you for reading **The Stepmother!**

COMING SOON! *The Search, Rebecca's Story #2.* If you'd like to be notified when it's available, **Visit Here:**

http://ticahousepublishing.subscribemenow.com

In the meantime, **are you wondering what to read next?** Why not read **The Lie? Here's a sample for you:**

Tessa Speicher threw herself on her bed and sobbed into her closed fists, trying to muffle the sound. Tears coursed down her face, puddling on the beautiful blue and yellow quilt.

It couldn't be true.

It simply *couldn't.*

But Tessa knew better. It was true all right. Calendars didn't lie. She drew her knees up to her chest, wishing she could die. There was no way she'd be able to face her mother with this. Life was hard enough without her father. The years since his death had been fraught with hardship.

But *this?*

This would be worse than anything that'd happened so far. Much, *much* worse. Tessa gulped back her tears. Feeling sorry for herself wouldn't help. Wishing for death wouldn't help. There was only one thing to do. Only one thing that might fix this mess.

She crawled off her bed and wiped her tears with her sleeve. She straightened her *kapp* and fanned her face, trying to dry her cheeks. Hopefully, her eyes weren't too swollen. If she were lucky, her mother wouldn't even be around. She'd be busy in the barn or busy in the kitchen, and there wasn't much chance Tessa would run into anyone else.

The tiny farm they'd leased didn't require extra help since they didn't farm the land. Somebody else leased the fields. Tessa and her mother made their living by selling milk and cheese to the *Englisch.*

It wasn't hugely profitable, but it paid the bills and kept a roof over their heads and food on the table.

Tessa crept down the stairs on bare feet, cautiously looking about as she went. No sign of her mother anywhere inside. If she slipped out the side door and ran around the back of the house and through the fields, she could leave without being detected.

But then what?

Was she going to march right up to Tom Miller's house and knock on the door? Ask his mother if he could come out and talk to her? There was no way she could do that; it simply wasn't done. But she *had* to talk to him. Urgently. Maybe, if she hid out by the side of the barn, she could catch him coming or going. That would probably be safest.

She left by the side door and scurried around the back of the house. When she got to the field, she ran as fast as she could toward the main road. Being early spring, the ground was cold on her bare feet, but she hardly noticed. All she could think of was finding Tom. Talking to Tom. Having Tom make this all better.

The Millers' farm was a short piece down the road. When she neared it, she carefully hid until she was on the road side of the barn. If she stayed back a bit, she could still see who was around, and unless they really looked, no one should see her. She leaned against the rough boards and caught her breath. She felt a surge of nausea rise to her throat, and she went completely still. She'd learned that if she didn't move a muscle when the nausea came, it would often pass without making her vomit.

She could hardly stand there on Miller land, retching her stomach out, now, could she?

Oh, Lord ... how had it come to this?

She lowered her head. She knew full well how it had come to this. She heard a noise and peered cautiously around the side of the barn. It was Tom's father, carrying a harness. She backed up and plastered herself against the wall.

Ten minutes or so later, she heard another sound. Then she heard a chuckle and a low voice talking to an animal, no doubt a horse. It was Tom. It had to be. She slithered forward and peered again around the barn to see Tom leading a pony toward the pony cart.

"Tom!" she whispered. "Tom! Over here!"

He paused and looked around. When he caught sight of her, his face crinkled into a wide grin. He looped the pony's reins over the cart and came to her.

"Tessa!" he said. "What are you doing here?"

He looked toward the road, as if checking for curious eyes, and then grabbed both her shoulders and kissed her soundly on the lips. "What a *gut* surprise."

She looked into his blue eyes and felt everything inside her relax. He loved her. He would make this right. Everything would work out now.

"Tom—" she started, but he interrupted her with another kiss.

"When can we see each other again?" he asked, his hands running up and down her arms.

"We're seeing each other now."

"You know what I mean."

"Tom..." Something in her expression must have alarmed him, because he went still, his gaze searching hers.

"What is it?"

"Do you love me?" she asked, hating the pleading sound in her voice.

"Of course, I do. How can you ask?"

"I mean *really* love me." She swallowed. "Can we be married?"

He blanched and stepped back an inch. "What? Now? You know we can't. We'll have to wait at least a year to be published. A year, at least. Until my *dat* leaves me the west fields. I told you this, Tessa."

"I know you did—"

"Then why are you pressuring me?" He frowned. "What's this about?"

"I-I'm with child."

He reared back as if she'd struck him, nearly losing his balance. *"What?"*

"I'm with child."

He stared at her. "How do you know?" He cringed. "Don't tell me you went to a doctor?"

"I don't need to. I've missed my monthlies. And I'm nauseated all the time. I just *know*."

"You can't be certain."

"Jah, I can." Why was he questioning her like this? She was right— there was no doubt in her mind.

"Then it's not mine."

She gaped at him. Black spots played around the edges of her vision, and she wavered. She would have fallen, had not Tom grabbed her and pushed her against the barn.

His expression was raw panic, and he stuck his face up against hers. "It's not mine. You hear? There's no way *Dat* will give me the west fields if he finds out you're pregnant. He'll call me a sinner and give the land to my brother. You know it's true."

"We *are* sinners, Tom. We are. Nothing can change that now." Tears burned in her eyes, and she felt them slip down her cheeks.

"*Nee. Nee.* I'm telling you, it's not mine. It can't be mine. It *mustn't* be mine." He let go of her and paced a circle in the dirt, kicking at the dust. He groaned and looked at her again. "I'll deny it. No one knows we've been seeing each other." His features grew rigid, and he backed further away from her.

"But, it *is* yours. And *we* know we've been seeing each other."

"No one's going to believe you. You and your *mamm* haven't been in our community that long. I've been here forever. The Millers have been here forever. They'll believe me."

Her knees buckled, and she slid down to the dirt. She rocked back and forth, biting her lip. This couldn't be happening. Tom loved her. He *did*. Otherwise, she would have never...

"You need to go now," he said stiffly, looking down at her. "Hurry. Before anyone sees you."

She glanced up through her tears. She didn't recognize him. His face was hard and twisted, and his eyes had gone cold. They looked almost ... evil.

"Tom..." she choked out.

"I'm sorry, Tessa," he said, his voice sharp and pointed. "I can't help you."

She shook her head as the tears continued to pour down her face. Her stomach roiled within her, and she felt vomit surge up her throat. She jerked her head to the side and heaved into the dirt. When she was finished, she was panting and dizzy.

"I have to go," Tom said. "I'm sorry, Tessa. I'm sorry..."

And he was gone. Tessa wiped her mouth with the back of her hand and stared at the spot where he'd just been. She was sinking, sinking fast into a murky black hole. There was nothing to grab onto. Nothing to break her fall. Darkness crept over her, and she could see no more.

VISIT HERE To Read More of *The Lie:*

http://ticahousepublishing.com/amish.html

Thank you for Reading

❧❀❧

If you **love Amish Romance, VISIT Here:**

http://ticahousepublishing.subscribemenow.com

to find out about all **New Hollybrook Amish Romance Releases! We will let you know as soon as they become available!**

If you enjoyed **_The Stepmother_** would you kindly take a couple minutes to leave a positive review on Amazon? It only takes a moment, and positive reviews truly make a difference. I would be so grateful! Thank you!

Turn the page to discover more Amish Romances just for you!

More Hollybrook Amish Romances
for You

❧❀❧

We love clean, sweet, rich Amish Romances and have a lovely library of Brenda Maxfield titles just for you! (Remember that ALL of Brenda's Amish titles can be downloaded FREE with Kindle Unlimited!) If you love bargains, you may want to start right here! Here is a sampling of our BARGAIN Box Sets!

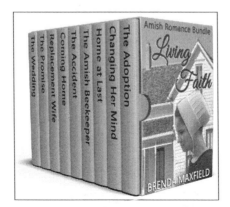

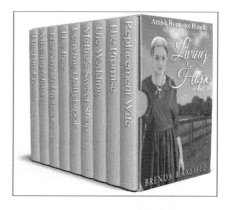

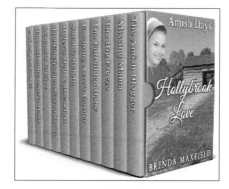

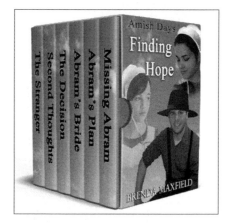

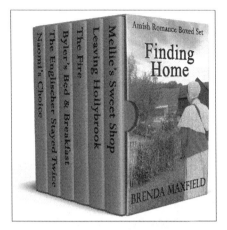

Here is the list of Brenda's single titles. They are conveniently grouped by our lovely Amish heroines. You're sure to find many favorites. Enjoy!

Hope's Story
Missing Abram
Abram's Plan
Abram's Bride

Sally's Story
The Decision
Second Thoughts
The Stranger

The Runaway

Josie's Story
The Schoolteacher's Baby
A Desperate Act

Marian's Story

The Amish Blogger

Missing Mama

The Big Freeze

A Loving Stranger

Annie's Story

The Forbidden Baby

Escaping Acre's Corner

Sarah's Return

Naomi's Story

Byler's Bed & Breakfast

The Englischer Stayed Twice

Naomi's Choice

Mellie's Story

Mellie's Sweet Shop

Leaving Hollybrook

The Fire

Faith's Story

The Adoption

Changing her Mind

Home at Last

Rhoda's Story

The Amish Beekeeper

The Accident

Coming Home

Emma's Story
The Deacon's Son
The Defiance
Emma's Decision

http://ticahousepublishing.com/amish.html

About the Author

My passion is writing! What could be more delicious than inventing new characters and seeing where they take you?

I am blessed to live in Indiana, a state I share with many Amish communities. (I find the best spices, hot cereal, and good cooking advice at an Amish store not too far away.)

I've lived in Honduras, Grand Cayman, and Costa Rica. One of my favorite activities is exploring other cultures. My husband, Paul, and I have two grown children and five precious grandchildren, three, special delivery from Africa and two, homegrown. I love to hole up in our lake cabin and write -- often with a batch of popcorn nearby. (Oh, and did I mention dark chocolate?)

I enjoy getting to know my readers, so feel free to write me at: contact@brendamaxfield.com. Subscribe to my Newsletter and get the latest news about releases:

http://ticahousepublishing.subscribemenow.com

Visit to learn about all my books: ticahousepublishing.com

Happy Reading!

www.ticahousepublishing.com

contact@brendamaxfield

Made in the USA
Columbia, SC
11 January 2019